Toots McGee

Toussaint 'Toots' William McGee is riding the chuck-lined-trail along the foothills of the Rocky Mountains when a sudden wave of dizziness propels him from the saddle and into oblivion.

When he wakes he is staring into the barrel of the rifle Sarah Baxter had used to ambush him, having mistaken his shaggy red hair and beard for those of Tom Danton, the man who had killed her family. Realizing her error she takes Toots home to recuperate where he learns of the family's plight and pledges his help.

But Danton and his men are ruthless and Toots must fight dirty if he is to save the Baxter ranch and the lovely woman who shot him.

Toots McGee

J.W. Throgmorton

A Black Horse Western

ROBERT HALE · LONDON

© J.W. Throgmorton 2014
First published in Great Britain 2014

ISBN 978-0-7198-1442-6

Robert Hale Limited
Clerkenwell House
Clerkenwell Green
London EC1R 0HT

www.halebooks.com

www.jwthrogmorton.com

Typeset by
Derek Doyle & Associates, Shaw Heath
Printed and bound in Great Britain by
CPI Antony Rowe, Chippenham and Eastbourne

CHAPTER 1

Absent warning or a reason for its cause, Toots felt a cold sweatiness drench over him. From far-off, the crack from a rifle reached his ears, but his brain did not make the connection. He swallowed hard to quell the urge to vomit. Wooziness made him unsteady, and he swayed in his saddle. In his mind, he stepped down with the intent to sit and rest a spell. In reality, he reeled and dropped from his horse landing like a sack of grain.

As if stabbed in the left shoulder by a white-hot poker, a fierce pain roused him. He dragged his sleeved arm across his eyes to remove the salty-sweat that burned them and blurred his vision. *My hat, where's my hat?* About his head, he searched the ground until he found his fur-felt Stetson. It'd cost him near a week's wages. It was the last thing off at night and first thing on in the morning.

Motionless, he narrowed his eyes to peer through the tall pines at the cloudless blue sky. The wince was involuntary; his shoulder screamed for attention. He bit down on the fingertips of his leather glove and slid it off his right-hand. His fingers eased to the source of the ache. High on his chest there was a sticky place the size of a silver dollar. His finger traced the ragged hole in his shirt. Through it, he could feel raw meat. It was numb to his touch; nevertheless, it throbbed in rhythm with his pulse.

After a moment, the haze in his mind cleared, *I've been shot.*

His eyes darted about. *Where'd the bushwhacker shoot from? Why hasn't he sent another slug my way? Maybe, he thinks he's done me in, and closin' in to make sure.*

With a cocked ear, he listened for the noise of someone's approach, but nothing sounded. *I wonder if I can stand.* He rolled on his right side and pushed up with his good arm. With his feet under him, he staggered to find cover behind the rocks and trees by the stream. Still no second shot, then it occurred to him, *maybe he can't see me off my horse.*

His pony, Knothead, the damnedest most stubborn horse he'd ever known, stood ground hitched by the stream. With his rider's movement, the mustang paint lifted its head and looked at him. With a nicker, he ambled over to where his rider crouched and nudged him for attention.

'Stupid horse,' he whispered. 'We're bein' shot at?'

With Knothead's lead tied to a sapling, Toots eased up to retrieve his saddle-bags and tossed them on the ground. Then, he shucked his long gun from its boot.

Nestled in the rocks, he pulled a clean shirt from his saddle-bags. Careful to take it from the front tail, he tore a section free. His mother always said, 'Waste not, want not'. He intended to wear the remains.

He bent to soak the cloth in the stream; his head began to spin, and then a sudden weakness. He nearly fell in. An involuntary and nimble left hand planted on the bank's edge kept him dry. However, the jolt to his shoulder racked it with pain, and he nearly fainted. A blob of blood oozed from the wound. With care, he rotated his shoulder; his muscles screamed for him to stop, but first he needed to confirm nothing was broken.

The cool crystal-clear water soothed the burn in his shoulder, the first relief he'd felt since stepping down from his pony. He lay back and closed his eyes.

He didn't pass out; he sort of nodded off. When his eyes opened there stood an angel. Dressed like a man in a poplin shirt and wool pants, they didn't conceal the soft curves of a beautiful young woman. She had a rifle aimed at him.

Yet there was no denying she looked like an angel. Her mussed coal-black hair hung passed her shoulders; chestnut eyes fringed with thick lashes stared at him; her jaw flexed and her thin lips formed a line across her face. She appeared determined to finish what she'd begun.

He asked, 'Am I dead?'

She levered the Winchester. 'You soon will be, Danton—'

His eyebrows squished together, then his situation became clear; he raised his good arm in protest. 'Whoa there! My name's McGee, Toots McGee, you got the wrong man.'

The angel's glare softened, and she began to laugh. 'Toots? Who ever heard of a man named Toots?'

McGee didn't hold with having his name laughed at; his red-beaded jaw clenched and his cheeks flushed. 'It's sort of a nickname,' he protested. 'My name is Toussaint William McGee.' The girl's expression didn't change. 'My mother is French, and my father Scottish. He's called William or Bill, and Toussaint bein' a mouth full, folks took to callin' me Toots. It stuck.'

Her brow pinched, as she studied his face. 'You're younger I reckon, but you do favor him. It's your shaggy red hair – stands out a good mile.' She lowered her rifle. 'I guess maybe I got the wrong galoot after all. Besides, Danton ain't smart enough to come up with a name like that.'

7

With her rife pointed elsewhere, his body's tension relaxed and left him feeling weak, but his anger lessened, too. He exhaled a long breath. He pulled at a lock of his hair. 'Like I said, my father is Scottish.' Her mode of dress made him curious. Why would she want to look like a man? 'Who's this fellow Danton you took me for?'

'Why Tom Danton, that's who; he's the low-down dirty buzzard that killed my pap and my brother.' After a breath, she added, 'He'd kill Ma and me too if he got the chance.'

Toots watched the girl's face as she spoke about Danton: it held an icy calm expression. It resembled a marble statue he saw at the White Elephant saloon in Denver, and her voice was just as cold. He could tell she wanted Tom Danton dead.

'If you don't mind my askin' . . . why?'

'Huh? Sorry, I was just—' Kindled by the subject matter, the girl let go and spoke her mind. 'Danton works for a polecat name of Web Griffin. He owns most of Charlo and a lot of the countryside, too. He wants our place, but Pap wouldn't sell, so he had Danton murder 'im and my brother too.'

He felt a sense of the injustice she'd experienced, and asked, 'What'd the sheriff say when you reported it?'

Her chin held high, she stared at him – her eyes flinty. Her face flushed and then just as quick her face relaxed and her loveliness returned. 'That's right. You don't know 'em.'

The initial numbing shock from his injury began to fade. His nostrils flared as he smiled through the pain and shook his head. 'It's my first time in these parts.'

She continued. 'The sheriff works for Griffin, plus there ain't no witnesses.'

'What'd I miss, girl?' asked Toots. 'Then how do you know it was Danton that killed 'em?'

Hands to her hips, brow raised, her eyes conveyed concern as if she were talking to a child who refused to understand. Her piteous smile was soft and sincere, but it stirred his anger; he said, 'It's a reasonable question—'

'I told you,' she said. 'Griffin wants our land, and Danton is his hired killer. It couldn't be more plain.'

He moved and then winced with pain. 'Oh,' she gasped, her voice filled with worry. 'I wasn't sure that I hit you. Is it very painful?' She stared. 'You don't seem too bad hurt?'

'Well I tell you, Miss. I've enjoyed many a better day.'

She knelt to examine his shoulder. 'There's not much blood – that's good. Let me help you get mounted, and we'll head for the ranch. Ma's pretty handy with a needle and thread.'

He nodded. Together, with assistance from a nearby rock, they managed to get him astride Knothead. She tied its lead rope to her saddle and led the way along the stream to the meadow. Though she rode at a slow pace, the jolts traveled up his spine to his shoulder. His breath sawed in and out between thin lips. It was all he could do to stay conscious.

They cleared a rise and halted. Toots gazed upon a long lush valley with plentiful tall green grass. On its high end was a small lake fed by the snowmelt that trickled from snow-capped peaks. The lake spawned a narrow river, which coursed its way down the lie of the valley. It ran beneath a bridge and became lost among trees at the far end.

He felt nauseous, his brow wet with perspiration, but his skin was cool and clammy to the touch. To his amazement, he remained coherent, he asked, 'How many acres?'

'Near 500,000 all told,' said the girl.

'With all this grass, why fence your livestock?'

Her shoulders lowered, as did her voice. 'That's all we've got left. The rest were rustled, and our cowhand's run off.

Chen Lee, our cook, is the only one left – besides Mama and me.'

'It's peaceful; why not let 'em free to feed on the grass?'

'I plan to,' her confident smile returned, 'but I have to circle the valley every mornin' to make sure there ain't no polecats waitin' to rustle 'em soon as I open the gate. That's what I was doin' when I spied you ridin' toward our place.'

Blackness closed in around Toots. He felt himself go limp.

When he came to, he lay on a bed. A quick scan of the room's doodads told him it belonged to a girl, the girl who dozed in a chair next to his bed. His shoulder felt better, but he couldn't move his arm. A glance revealed they had bandaged it tight to his body. He realized his shirt was off, and he felt exposed, so he raised the covers and peeked; his pants were gone, too.

'Ahem,' he cleared his throat.

The girl's eyes opened wide; the whites were clear and enriched the beauty of their chestnut color. In the bright light, he thought he could see a hint of yellow. She gave him a warm smile. 'Good, you're awake. Hungry?'

When he stopped to think about it, he felt starved. 'I could eat my horse, if it was cooked.'

She laughed. It was genuine; her cheeks pinked, and though he found it hard to believe, her laughter made her even prettier. 'Your horse is safe. Chen fried chicken last night, would you like some?'

Toots looked out the window. It seemed earlier than when they arrived. His brow pinched, he asked, 'What happened?'

With a matter-of-fact attitude, she said, 'You dropped off your horse, so I came down here and got a wagon. Chen and

10

I brought you back home. Mama saw to your wounds and we've been waitin' for you to wake up.'

He began to put the pieces together. 'When was all this – and who removed my clothes?'

'Yesterday,' she said. He held his breath waiting for her to answer his other question. 'Mama and Chen.'

When he sighed his relief, she added, 'You ain't got anythin' I haven't seen before – I had a grown brother you know.'

Toots's face grew red. 'That may be, but I ain't him.'

She tugged at his cover, and laughed when he slammed his arm down to hold them tight. She stood. 'I'll get you something to eat.' Toots watched her backside as she sashayed out of the room and decided he could get used to women wearing pants.

An older woman, whose resemblance to the girl was remarkable, entered the room carrying a tray. She placed the tray on a small table beside the bed.

As he struggled to sit up, she stepped nearer. 'Here, let me help you.' With gentle strength, she lifted him and stuffed several pillows behind him for support. Her smell of flowers, cooking, and womanhood was pleasant. It reminded him of home.

She stood composed with her hands crossed on the front of her dress. 'There, that's better.' She paused for a breath. 'Mr McGee, I'm Mrs Helen Baxter. Sarah, my daughter, you've already met and Chen Lee, our cook, you'll meet later.'

Toots's belly gurgled, and he glanced at the tray of food. Her eyes followed. 'Oh dear,' she said, 'how rude of me.' She sat the tray on his lap and returned to her pose. 'Well – go ahead and eat.' Then her eyes widened with concern as she leaned toward him. 'Do you need my help?'

11

'No, ma'am.' He picked up a chicken leg and tore off a bite. After he'd cleaned the bones, she brought in buttered biscuits with honey drizzled atop and a cup of hot coffee. He smelled how strong it was when she placed the cup on his tray. He wolfed down the biscuits and leaned back on his pillows to savor the coffee.

Helen watched him eat; her eyes seemed to look through him as her lips curled at the corners of her mouth. When he finished, she asked, 'Can I get you anything else?' He shook his head. She gave him a wistful glance. 'I guess it's the mother in me, but I miss watching Luke and his father relish a meal. Men do seem to enjoy food ever so much more than women.'

As before, she held her hands crossed against her dress; she walked the distance of the bed. When she turned, her hands were balled into white knuckled fist. 'Ahem.' She paused, but only for a moment. 'I – no, we'd like you to know that we're very sorry that Sarah shot you. We want you to stay here until you're healed.' Her brow creased, her eyes glistened, and her face grew taut as she waited for him to respond.

'I understand, ma'am. Your daughter explained your situation – I'm powerful sorry about your husband and son.'

Helen's face sank, and she gave him a pensive smile. She stepped next to the bed and patted his good shoulder. 'Thank you.' She stared briefly out the window. She dabbed a tear with her handkerchief, collected the tray, and left his room.

Now that he was alone, Toots surveyed the room again. He remembered that the house was log-built, probably from the timbers nearby. Sarah's room seemed spacious, and the east-facing window made the room light and airy. The painted furniture was white, and a wool rug covered most of

12

the wooden floor. In the room's far corner was a small cast-iron stove to keep her room cozy in the winter. Feeling drowsy, he laid back.

When his eyes opened to darkness, he realized he'd been asleep. He needed to get up so he pushed on the table beside the bed for support. It tipped and tumbled across the floor as he flopped back on the bed; Chen and Helen rushed into the room. Toots used the bedding to cover himself.

Helen asked, 'What were you trying to do?'

She and Chen helped him back into bed. Resituated, he said, 'I need to get up, where are my clothes?'

Chen spoke for the first time. 'Your clothes are drying on a line. In the meantime,' he glanced at Helen, who nodded, 'may I suggest we see if one of Mr Baxter's nightshirts would fit?' Helen hurried away and returned with several articles of clothing, including a nightshirt.

With Chen's help, Toots got into the shirt. Luke Baxter was bigger than him, so there was plenty of room for him and his bandaged shoulder. Now that he was on his feet, he felt better and wanted to explore the house. Chen escorted him from Sarah's room out to the main living space, through the dining area, and into the kitchen where he could sit at the table.

'Would you like something to eat?' asked Chen. 'Supper is done, but I'm sure I can find something.'

'Just some coffee please, if there is any, Mr Lee.'

The Chinaman paused to look Toots up and down; his face relaxed into a smile. 'Yes there is plenty and it's freshly brewed, Mr McGee.'

Toots studied the old man, who seemed a cross between Eastern and Western cultures; the Chinaman spoke English better than Toots, and wore western-style clothing. His fine white-hair was braided into a pigtail that hung to his waist, and his gossamer beard grew down to the center of his chest. On his head, he wore a black-silk skullcap.

At length, he smiled at the old man. 'Please call me Toots.'

Chen nodded. 'You may address me as Chen.' He turned, and busied himself at the stove. When he came back to the table, he brought coffee, and also cold biscuits with a dollop of homemade apple jelly. Despite his earlier denial of hunger, he gobbled down the biscuits with a relished satis-faction.

'Chen, if you'll allow it, I got a question.'

Chen nodded, giving Toots a patient smile.

'You wear America clothes, but you've a pigtail. I've seen Chinamen in Denver, and their hair was cut short like mine.'

'Confucius says, "Hair is part of our skin and should never be cut".'

Toots's forehead creased as he tried to recall if he'd ever heard the name. 'Confucius?' he asked.

Chen smiled. His eyes twinkled with amusement. Finally, he said, 'Confucius was a teacher who lived before the time of your Christ. Many of us Chinese follow his teachings.'

'Oh – like the Mormons?'

'Not quite. . . .' he said, but added nothing more.

An hour later, Sarah came in from her last chore of the day; driving their herd to the pens for safekeeping. She came through the kitchen door, hung her hat on a peg, removed her spurs, and untied her chaps. Her movements were slow and labored. The circles under her eyes denoted her exhaustion.

Toots wondered how much longer she could continue

with her up-at-dawn-and-work-till-sunset pace; he guessed not long.

He and Chen shared a look. Toots nodded toward Sarah, and in a low tone, he asked, 'How long has this been goin' on?'

Concern for Sarah shone in Chen's eyes as he answered. 'Mr Baxter and little Luke were murdered six weeks back. The cattle started to go missing shortly after. The rustling stopped when Sarah began her nightly roundups; I'd say about four weeks ago.'

Toots glanced once more over his shoulder at Sarah as she went back outside to wash up. 'She's not goin' to last much longer, Chen. Isn't there anyone she can hire to help out?'

'None,' said Chen, 'they're all afraid of Griffin's men.'

Sarah returned to the kitchen. At the table, she dropped on to a chair, and her head flopped on to her crossed arms.

'Would you like coffee, Sarah?' asked Chen.

'I'd like to sleep for a week, but I guess coffee will have to do.' She sat up to take the cup Chen offered, and seemed to notice Toots, she asked, 'Should you be out of bed?'

'Sleepin' for a week ain't all it's cracked up to be. So, I got Chen to help me into the kitchen.' When she smiled, she didn't appear as tired as earlier; maybe it was the coffee. 'I was hopin' to eat supper with your family – if that's all right.'

'We're happy to have you join us,' said Helen, who'd just entered. 'New conversation at supper is always welcomed.' She stood by her daughter. 'Are you all right, Sarah, you look so tired. You take the bed tonight – I'll sleep on the pallet.'

Toots looked from one to the other. 'You've been sleepin' on the floor on account of I took your bed?'

Sarah's mouth curled up at its corners. 'I'd say that's the

15

least I can do since it was my bullet that put you there.'

His eyes went wide, his lips parted as if to speak. His sense of chivalry stirred to its core. 'Mrs McGee raised her son better 'an that. If anybody sleeps on the floor—'

Helen spoke, her voice held a sharp edge, 'You'll do no such thing, and that's final.'

Toots clenched his jaw and his face flushed red. 'Ma'am, I'm sorry to be disrespectful, but I can't oblige you on this.' He paused, his face softened as an idea flashed in his mind. 'Where'd your son sleep? I can bed down there?'

Chen spoke up, 'In the bunkhouse with the hands and me.'

Toots's green eyes gleamed with satisfaction, as he grinned. 'That's settled then – I'll move out there after supper.'

Helen said, 'But—'

Chen interrupted, 'It'll be fine, Mrs Baxter, I'll be out there with him, and if I need you I'll call.'

Helen glanced at Sarah, who sat slumped with her eyes closed. 'All right, I'll agree for Sarah's sake and no other reason. Chen, will you please help me get her room ready?'

By the time they returned, Sarah's head had returned to her crossed arms on the table. Though she stood and walked between Chen and Helen, Toots doubted she'd recall it in the morning.

Later in the bunkhouse, Toots asked Chen, 'Would you help me change my bandage? I'd like to fix it so all I need is a sling. That way I can put on my clothes and move around some.'

Chen stared at him. 'It's only been three days—'

'It'll be fine. Mrs Baxter sewed them holes up tight, so I should be able to move around without botherin' 'em none.'

16

The next morning at breakfast, Helen's expression showed surprise when she saw Toots fully dressed, gun-belt and all. She scowled at Chen. 'You had something to do with this.'

Chen shrugged. 'He knows his own mind.'

'Ma'am, you did a good job of sewin' me up. I'll be careful.' She put her hands on her hips and frowned as Toots eased his arm from the sling, and slowly moved it about. He added, 'Besides, it'll get stiff if I leave it bound up like that, and I need both my arms.' At length, she gave in and smiled.

Breakfast done, Toots went out to check on Knothead. He pranced to the gate and hung his head over for Toots to scratch behind his ears. 'You don't look no worse for wear.' Knothead whinnied and nudged Toots. 'You'd like to get out and stretch your legs – that it, boy?' He stroked his horse's neck. 'Me too—'

Toots spent the day with his arm out of the sling to work the stiffness from his shoulder. At supper, he removed the sling and fended for himself, parsing his food with his knife and fork.

Helen and Sarah looked on. Helen's gaze held concern, she asked, 'Don't you think you're rushing things with your arm?'

'No, ma'am. I plan to give it a week or two before putting it to real use, but it needs movement to stay limber.'

'I see—' Her expression said she wasn't convinced.

'I was thinkin' if Chen helps me with my saddle, I'll ride the circuit tomorrow so Sarah could sleep in, then I'd help with the cattle in the evenin' – the work would go twice as fast.'

'I appreciate the offer,' said Sarah, 'but you still have some mendin' to do, and—'

17

'I got to take Knothead out one way or the other, so you might as well let me combine it with a chore.'

His easy grin plus her tiredness won out. 'Since you put it that way, thanks, I accept.'

Helen asked, 'Do I hear a Texas accent in your voice. How long have you been in Montana?'

Toots grinned and a bit of color came to his cheeks. 'I come up from Texas in sixty-nine with one of the early cattle drives. I weren't more 'an seventeen, but these big o' Montana skies grabbed hold of me and I've been here ever since.'

Sarah hunched forward and focused on Toots. 'That was almost five years ago. What've you been doin' since?'

His eyes beamed at them as he warmed to the subject of Montana. 'I've been seein' the territory from one end to the other and top to bottom. There's always a job for a good hand.'

CHAPTER 2

The next morning, their routine began. Thereafter, it adjusted daily with Toots taking over more and more of the work. Things had been quiet and Toots began to consider leaving the stock out overnight, but then he saw the riders.

'Sarah,' her mother called, 'it's time to get up.' She sprang out of bed and climbed into her clothes fast as she might and rushed into the kitchen. 'Something quick, Mama, I've got the stock to tend to.'

'Toots already put them out to pasture. Sit down. Chen is preparing your breakfast.'

Sarah sighed and rolled her eyes. 'We can't let Toots do all my chores. It's not right.'

'Sarah, Toots is an experienced ranch hand. I don't wish to hurt your feelings, but he does the work faster, and doesn't seem to get as exhausted.' Helen paused. 'I guess we've got an employee – mind you, I don't approve of your selection methods.'

The twinkle in her eyes and the wide grin on her mother's face made Sarah blush when she looked up. 'Mama, that's mean. I've said I was sorry for shootin' Toots.'

'I know, dear, but since he's arrived things seem to be better. You're less tired, and your mood has improved. I just

19

couldn't resist the tease.'

Chen placed a plate in front of Sarah. 'The young man's made our lives a good deal more comfortable. We need more like him.'

'I suppose we should speak with him tonight about his wages,' said Helen. 'Though I'm not sure how we'll be able to pay him.'

Chen said, 'If you'd allow me, I have money saved.'

Helen stared at Chen, her mouth made a thin line and her eyes flashed. 'Chen, I would never impose on you. That's your money, and you've earned it. I wished we could've paid you more.'

'Mrs Baxter, you need to think about this. You need money to keep the ranch. If you're not able to hold on to the ranch, then I don't have a place to live. At my age, I doubt I'd last long on my own. So, my providing the money you need to set things right is a purely selfish act on my part.'

'Mama, Chen is family. If he needed your help, you wouldn't think an instant on it. You'd do whatever he needed.'

She saw the single-mindedness in her mother's face soften. Finally, Helen sighed. 'Oh all right but you won't just give us the money. You'll be part owner of the ranch. Agreed?'

'If that's what you wish, Mrs Baxter.'

'Chen, will you call me Helen now that we're partners?'

His face was placid, unreadable. 'I think not, Mrs Baxter.'

Helen's face fell and she looked away.

'Mrs Baxter, you're asking me to change traditions that have been engrained in my culture for thousands of years. Please believe me, I appreciate your sentiment, but I'm happier with addressing you as Mrs Baxter.'

Chen's brow pinched, and his eyes pleaded with Helen to comprehend. She looked at him, uncertain; finally, she smiled and said, 'I think I understand.'

His composure returned, Chen left the kitchen and returned with a leather pouch. 'There is two thousand dollars in there,' he said. 'Will that be adequate?'

'I should say so. If we can get Griffin to leave us alone we could set the ranch right again.'

Sarah asked, 'How were you able to save so much?'

Chen smiled. 'My needs are few. Your father paid me every month just like the ranch hands.' He chuckled. 'I had no need to rush off to town and spend my wages.' He held out his hands as explanation for the rest of his possible comments.

The sound of gunfire halted conversation; they all rushed outside and scanned the countryside toward the sound.

Toots saw the men first. One of them pointed in his direction, and all galloped toward him. He held the high ground, so he shucked his Winchester, grabbed a box of ammunition, his canteen, and dismounted. He tied Knothead and returned to his position just as the four men reached the incline.

They must have assumed he'd lit out, like fools they started up the hill. The shaggy red-hair of the lead rider identified him. Toots didn't see a resemblance other than their hair color. So that's Danton. Toots took aim at a rock a few yards ahead of Danton and squeezed the trigger. After the spray of rock shards followed by the crack of his long gun, they emptied their saddles and scurried for cover.

Danton called, 'Do you know who you're shootin' at?'

Toots chuckled, and said, 'I reckon I do, you're Tom Danton – the back shootin' bastard, who murdered Mr

21

Baxter and his boy.'

In their panic, none of them had had the sense to grab their rifles when they bailed, so they fired away with their handguns. The bullets fell short by ten yards.

Toots fired four quick shots at their horses, and they bolted. 'This is your only warnin',' called Toots, 'show your faces around here again, and I'll shoot to kill – now get!'

Finally, three of the men stood with their hands in the air. They waited, staring up at Toots, who kept them in his sights. At length, they turned and started after their animals.

'You too, Danton,' called Toots.

Danton called, 'Cowboy, you ain't seen the last of me.'

Toots stood and lowered his Winchester; he was out of Danton's revolver range. 'The name's McGee.'

Danton rose, holstered his revolver, and backed away to the cover of trees before he turned. When they were out of sight, Toots took Knothead and worked his way around above, where he could watch them. He intended to stay there until they caught their horses before he rode back to the ranch.

They waited on the porch. There'd been no further shooting after the initial fusillade. Helen clung to her daughter, she asked, 'Do you think they killed him?'

'I don't know, Mama, but I intend to find out. Chen, would you please get my rifle and things while I saddle my horse?'

As Chen turned, Helen said, 'Sarah, wait—' She took Sarah's hand into hers. 'Please wait. If they've killed Toots, there's nothing you can do for him. If he's alive, he'll return.'

Sarah's jaw was set; there would be no changing her mind. She glanced at Chen, who nodded, and then ran to

22

the barn. When she came out, Chen stood on the porch with her rifle and canteen. He passed her a knotted sack. 'If he's all right, he'll be hungry.'

Her mother stepped forward. 'Sarah, please be careful, you're all I have left.' With a handkerchief snatched from her sleeve, she blotted away her tears, and then forced a brave smile.

Sarah galloped away toward the tree line where the sound of shooting had come from. Within twenty minutes, she crested the ridge that divided the valley from the woodlands. Fear that he wouldn't be there conflicted with the fear that he'd be there but hurt, or worse.

With her rifle laid across her saddle's rise, she walked her horse along the ridge. To one side, she could see the whole grassy valley that was home, wooded hills beyond, and in the far distance the dusty purple of the Great Rocky Mountains. Below her were dense woodlands, dotted with glens where outcroppings blocked the trees. She searched for a sign of Toots.

As she rode, she thought of what he'd come to mean to her and her family. His arrival gave them hope; they'd begun to think that maybe they had a chance to beat Griffin. A realization came to Sarah; she'd begun to think of Toots as someone permanent in her life. He certainly wasn't dashing like the men in the novels she read, but he wasn't unattractive either.

She kept to the shade of the pine trees, where the fallen needles muted the clip-clop of her horse's approach. When she called, Toots jumped with a start. He turned, smiled, and waved for her to join him.

As she rode toward him, she decided that in his way, he was handsome, rough-hewn maybe, but still fetching. His mop of red-hair needed a trim, but he had a nice face, broad shoulders, and he was a good man. His green eyes were like gems at which she couldn't stop staring.

'What was the shootin'?' she asked.

He pointed to the trail below; two of the men had caught their mounts and chased after the other horses. Danton stood looking in their direction. She wondered if he could see them.

Toots must have read her thoughts. 'I don't think he can see us, but he knows I'm here watchin' to make sure he leaves.'

'Are you goin' to tell me what happened?'

He glanced at her, his smile warm and caring, and then he turned back to watch Danton's progress. All four were mounted, and they rode away. 'Nothin' much,' he said. 'Them jaspers come lookin' for trouble and they found it – that's all.'

Sarah studied his expression and then looked deep into his chartreuse green eyes; a tinge of yellow gleamed with the sun's light. She saw only a calm resolution, a conviction that spoke to a determination. Her pap would've said this man had grit.

'There were so many shots, how come no one was hurt?'

Toots chuckled. 'I was the only one with a rifle, and I didn't shoot to kill.'

'Mother and Chen are worried – we should get home.'

He shook his red shaggy mane. 'I want to stay here a while to make sure they don't double back. I'll be along soon enough.'

Sarah sighed. 'I suppose you're right, but come home soon as you can.' She reined her horse toward the ranch, then stopped and turned back to Toots. 'Chen thought you might be hungry and sent this.' She handed him the flour sack of food and then headed toward the ranch. She

24

thought about what she'd said. *Why did I say it just that way: 'get home'?*

The ridge behind her, she galloped back to the ranch. As she neared, she saw Chen and her mother still on the porch, but now they were armed. Chen held a Winchester and her mother had her father's double-barreled Lang.

'Chen, Mama, what do you two think you're doin'?'

Helen's brow wrinkled, and her tone was stern. 'What does it look like? We've armed ourselves in case Griffin's men attack.'

'Mama, do you even know how to fire Pap's Lang?'

'I do. I'll have you know that I'm a pretty fair markswoman and not to be trifled with, and before you embarrass yourself with Chen: yes, he can shoot that Winchester.' She looked to Chen and back to Sarah. 'Before you and your brother were born this was a tough land. We've shot more than one Indian off his pony when they came looking for trouble.'

Sarah had never really thought about what it must have been like when her mother and father first came to Montana. Though she'd had a lot to consider these last weeks since Pap and little Luke's murders, her parents' early life wasn't included.

'Toots will be along later,' said Sarah. 'He's watchin' to make sure Danton and his men leave.'

Helen cradled the shotgun. 'I've got things that need tended to.' She left Chen and Sarah on the porch.

Chen sat down on a porch rocker and laid the rifle across the chair's arms. Sarah perched on the railing in front of him and stared; she saw Chen in a new light.

He returned her stare. 'What is it, Sarah?'

Sarah's face relaxed and she smiled at him warmly. 'I reckon I don't really know you – I mean know very much about you.' Her eyes lit with curiosity. 'I know Pap saved your life and all, but how did that come to be?'

He took a deep breath and issued a large sigh. 'It has been many years since I've thought about those days.'

Sarah leaned forward. 'Please tell me about those days.'

'Nearly thirty years ago in China, my English and administrative skills were highly sought, so I found employment with a prominent British family living in Hong Kong.'

'Oh, what were they like?'

'They were just a family; I hadn't worked for them long before I was taken.'

Sarah's eyes grew wide, she spoke in a low tone. 'Taken? You mean you were kidnapped?'

Chen chuckled at her reaction to his story. He looked to his left then right, and with an air of conspiracy said, 'They called it being shanghaied. I was on a business errand at the docks for my employer. Several men attacked me, and the next thing I knew I found myself robbed and aboard a ship at sea.'

'How did you meet Pap?' she asked, 'Did he help you escape?'

Chen held up his hand to quiet the girl's peppering of questions. 'In truth, it was nothing that exciting. I slipped off the ship in San Francisco. Your father was at the docks loading freight bound for Denver. I hid in his wagon; he didn't find me until we were on the road. After I explained my situation, he offered to take me with him if I was willing to help him with the work, and of course, I agreed.'

Her disappointment was clear when she asked, 'That's how he saved your life? He gave you a ride?'

Chen laughed with delight at Sarah's reaction. 'That was a huge thing. He could have put me off the wagon, or taken me to collect a reward, but he didn't. Instead he took me east with him to Denver. Along the way, we became friends.'

'Oh,' said Sarah and she rose to leave.

'. . . but Carson City was altogether different,' said Chen.

Sarah halted mid-step and returned to the railing. Her eyes looked at Chen with eager brilliancy 'Well?' she said.

'When I arrived to America, I discarded the sailor's garments the crew wore, and put on my changshan and cap—'

Sarah said, 'That's the black silk clothes from China—right?'

Chen nodded and continued. 'When we arrived in Carson City we stopped at the hotel for the night. Chinese weren't welcome there, so your father claimed I was his servant. The hotel gave in and gave us rooms. Later, at the saloon—'

'Ahem.' They both looked up to see Helen listening from the doorway. 'The less gory version if you please, Chen.'

Chen smiled and bowed his head. 'Two men, who were quite drunk, took exception with my attire. They said I was more attractive than the girls who work at the saloon. Your father stepped in and they let me alone. The next morning, he bought me American style clothing, which I've worn ever since.'

'But how did Pap stop them from botherin' you?'

'Sarah,' said Helen. 'That's enough. Let Chen be.'

'Mama—' Sarah's eyes pleaded. 'If Pap was a hero, I want to know the details. I'm a grown-up now. Don't treat me like a child.'

Helen sighed. Her eyes rolled with exasperation, she looked at Chen and shrugged. He smiled and glanced at Sarah, who'd regained her perch on the rail. Helen remained at the doorway. It was obvious that she wanted to hear about adventure too.

'There is much more to tell,' said Chen. 'One of the two

men grabbed me. Your father jumped to his feet and struck the man square in the face, knocking him to the floor. The other man reach for his revolver and your father drew his first and shot the man dead. As the man fell, the first man reached for his gun, so your father killed him too. It was over before it started. I've worked for your father ever since.'

Helen asked, 'Are you satisfied now, Sarah?'

She sprang off the rail. 'Pap was a gunfighter?'

'Now, Sarah, that's why I didn't want Chen to tell you the details. I knew you'd get the wrong impression. Your father was not a gunfighter. He was a businessman and rancher, who was brave and fought if need be; a lot of men were in those days.'

Sarah turned to Chen. 'It's a fine thing to know about Pap. Thank you for telling me.' She beamed at her mother, and her eyes shined with pride as she walked into the house.

Chen called after her, 'Here comes Toots.'

Sarah returned to the porch in time to see him riding across the field, rifle in hand.

CHAPTER 3

With a slow easy gait, Knothead carried Toots to the ranch house porch; flushed with excitement he gave them a wide grin. A twitch of the reins brought the horse to a halt and he sprang from the saddle.

Sarah's grin pushed her cheeks up, and her sparkling eyes formed crescents as she watched him dismount. 'They're gone?'

Toots nodded then turned to Chen. 'That dab of food you sent was welcomed. Any chance I could have some more?'

Helen took charge. 'As much as you want.' She too smiled broadly. 'Come into the kitchen. Chen, please see to his horse?'

'That's not necessary, ma'am,' said Toots, 'I'll be ridin' out later to see that the range remains clear.'

Helen searched Toots's face. 'Do you expect trouble?'

'No, ma'am. It just makes good sense to be careful.' He paused. 'Ain't there no one we could count on to work with us?'

Helen's face saddened. 'I'm afraid not, Toots. Our men deserted us after my husband and son were murdered.'

'What about Gus Wallace?' asked Sarah. 'He would've

stayed if you'd asked him to?'

'Gus Wallace?' asked Toots.

'Yup, he's a good hand too,' said Sarah, 'I think he's sweet on Mama – that's why she wouldn't ask him to stay.'

'Sarah!' said Helen, her voice filled with warning. 'You know that's not true. I can't ask someone to risk their life for us.'

'Toots is riskin' his!'

Helen sighed, and gave a half-hearted laugh. 'So he is, and that reminds me – Toots, we haven't talked about your wages.'

Toots smiled, his faced flushed. 'Ma'am, I've got money in my pocket and I know things are tight for you. You don't have to worry about my wages.'

'No such thing,' said Helen. 'You're working for the ranch, so you'll be paid. Now how much?'

'Thirty and found is usual, ma'am,' offered Toots.

'Chen, what did my husband pay our foreman?'

Chen nodded agreement. 'Fifty a month, Mrs Baxter.'

'Then it's fifty dollars a month – you're the new foreman.'

He exhaled a long breath, looked down, and worked his boot heel into the ground. He'd never been foreman before. He believed he could do the job well enough, but he never wanted the responsibility, and it meant he'd be tied to a single place. He glanced at Sarah; her eager smile made him swallow hard, so he decided to do it. He'd do it for Sarah and her family.

'Where can I find Gus Wallace?' said Toots.

Sarah stood next to her mother. 'Hot damn, he's gonna stay.'

Helen's mouth fell open as she turned to her daughter. 'That's enough of that kind of talk.' She crossed her arms and bore down on Sarah, causing her to lean backward. 'I've let you hang around the cowhands too long. Worse, I haven't corrected your way of speaking, but it changes today. Is that understood?'

Sarah's face burned red. 'Yes, Mother,' she said. 'I am sorry for the crude language, and I will work on how I speak.'

Helen's face softened and her eyes glistened. 'I'm sorry, Sarah, but you do know better, and now that you're a young woman, your speech says a lot about the type of person you are.'

Toots stepped away. After their voices softened, he returned to the house.

'Ahem.' They turned. 'Where's Gus Wallace?'

Still red faced from the scolding, Sarah said, 'Mr Wallace made reference to finding employment at the Roberts' ranch. It is forty miles east of here – I think.'

He rubbed his face as he considered; he needed to shave. 'Do you reckon you can handle things for a couple of days while I ride over there to palaver with him?'

Sarah put her hands on her hips and stomped toward him, her mother's scolding forgotten. 'I was takin' care of 'em before you came, so I reckon I can do it while you're gone.'

Helen shook her head and sighed. 'Sarah, your speech—'

She drew back. 'Sorry, Mother.' To Toots she said, 'We will be fine.' Her smile was demure and she batted her lashes. 'But, please, do hurry back – you're needed.' This time it was Toots who blushed, and then everyone burst into laughter.

At sun-up, with directions from Sarah, Toots headed east for the Robert's Rocking-R ranch. It was late morning when he arrived at the main house. A few hands milled around the

31

barn and corral. They stopped what they were doing when he rode up.

The Roberts' ranch appeared to be a successful operation. The main house was two-story and sided with white clapboards. All the double hung windows were open and curtains of varies colors fluttered in the breeze. The covered porch wrapped at least three sides of the house, as that was all Toots could see.

A grey-haired broad shouldered man sat on a rocker smoking his pipe. He stood and moved his lanky frame to the steps where Toots reined Knothead. Close up, the man's face looked like wrinkled fine leather with intense blue eyes beneath bushy white eyebrows. He pushed up his hat, knocked out his pipe, and then said, 'Sorry, son, but I ain't hirin'.'

Toots tapped the brim of his hat. 'Mr Roberts?' The old man nodded. 'I'm McGee, foreman for the Baxter place near Charlo—'

'I know it.' Roberts repacked his pipe, but he didn't light it. 'What's it got to do with me?'

A few of the hands moseyed over to listen. Toots scanned the men, but didn't recognize anyone. He was not used to public speaking, but now wasn't the time to falter. 'Have you heard about the trouble they been havin'?'

Again, Roberts nodded. 'It's too bad. Web Griffin ought to be hung for killing Baxter and the boy.'

'I agree, sir, but in the meantime, I'm tryin' to locate a fella name of Gus Wallace – I heard he was workin' for you.'

Roberts didn't respond immediately. Toots could tell he was trying to size him up; it wasn't the first time a ranch owner gave him the once over, and probably wouldn't be the last. He waited patiently.

At length, the old man said, 'Yup, he works for me – him and a few others from Baxter's. What's your business with Wallace?'

Toots shifted in his saddle, he dreaded the old man's reaction, but he had to be honest, 'I'm here to offer him a job – the other men too, if they'll come.'

The old man's jaw clenched tight, and his eyes squinted. He stared at Toots for near a full minute, and then he relaxed and put his pipe between his teeth and lit it up. After several puffs, the coal burned even. 'I'll tell you what – you go ahead and ask, and if they want to go, I'll let 'em. Shucks, I'll even hold their jobs for 'em in case things don't work out.'

Toots exhaled. Until then, he hadn't realized that he'd been holding his breath. He grinned at the old man. 'Thank you, sir.'

'One more thin',' said Roberts. 'I like your grit, son. If things don't work out, you've got one too – if you survive.'

Still smiling, Toots tapped his hat and reined Knothead toward the bunkhouse. As he rode up, a rawboned man in his early fifties filled the doorway. The man's sandy-brown hair topped a rugged brow; intense blue eyes stared at him. Beneath a bushy grey beard, Toots noted his ruddy complexion of broken veins that testified to his years spent living outdoors.

Smoke drizzled from a cigarette dangling from his lip causing one eye to squint. The man said, 'Boys tell me you're ridin' for the Box-B. That right?' His gravelly voice made Toots think that some of the broken veins were from too much whiskey.

Toots tilted back his hat and hung his leg over the saddle horn for comfort. A wry smile came to his face. 'Bunkhouse telegraph's quick – you Gus Wallace?'

33

The man nodded. Toots said, 'Mrs Baxter sends her regards.'

Wallace's eyes brightened when he heard her name. 'Is Mrs Baxter doin' all right?'

Toots looked at the man and saw that it wasn't just conversation, the man truly wanted to know. 'She's doin' fine. So is Sarah and the Chinaman.'

Wallace nodded, his relief visible. 'What do you want here?'

'I'm foreman for the Box-B and I've come to see if you're willin' to come back and work for us again.'

Wallace studied Toots. 'You're kinda young to be a foreman.'

Toots let the comment pass. 'Mrs Baxter's got the money to pay wages. If there's gunplay with Danton and Griffin I expect there'll be somethin' extra come the end of the month.'

'You expectin' trouble with Danton?'

Toots smiled. 'I sent him packin' once, so I figure he'll be back lookin' for trouble. I aim to give him more 'an he can handle, but we need men. You game?'

The wrinkles at the corners of Wallace's eyes deepened as he peered at Toots. Finally, he said, 'Big Mose and Little Mose come here with me. You want them too?'

'If they're willin', but I don't want no misunderstandin'. There's likely to be gunplay.'

Gus looked up to Toots. 'We was willin' to stay before, but Mrs Baxter wouldn't let us. She was powerful upset about losin' her husband and little Luke.' Wallace paused, and pulled a bandanna from his pocket and blew his nose. 'She set a great store by that boy – it liked to've kilt her when he died. Truth be told, we liked Mr Baxter too. The boy an' Sarah was always underfoot, but they was good kids, so we

34

didn't mind none.'

Toots grinned. 'Is that a yes?'

'Son, that's the most words I ever spoke at one time. Hell yes, it's yes. Give us time to collect our personables and say our goodbyes to Mr Roberts and we'll be ready to leave.'

Less than an hour later, they headed west towards the Box-B. Six in all, Big Nose Karl and Pete Johnson, Civil War veterans itchin' for some adventure and extra pay decided to come along. Wallace vouched for them, so Toots agreed.

Late afternoon, Toots and the crew rode up to the house. Sarah bound through the door and off the porch with child-like glee. 'Gus, you came back.' She scanned the other faces. 'Big Mose, and Little Mose, you too. This is wonderful.' She called, 'Mama, they're here, they're here, come see!'

Helen, followed by Chen, came out on to the porch. A warm glow came to her eyes when she saw their rough unshaven faces.

Gus pulled his sweat-stained hat from his head and nodded towards Helen. 'Howdy, Mrs Baxter. We're right happy to be back.' His grin was toothy and meant only for Helen. A bit more subdued, he turned to Sarah and added, 'You too, Miss Sarah.' He nodded to Chen, who bowed slightly in return.

The rest of the men tapped their hats and nodded. They sat for a prolonged period. Finally, Gus reined his mount toward the bunkhouse. All but Toots followed. He dismounted and came into the house.

'Well, we've got some hands.'

Chen followed everyone into the house. 'I need to go to town for supplies. We haven't enough food to keep that bunch fed.'

'Can it wait a day?' asked Toots. 'I can ride in with you.'

35

'That will not be necessary, Toots. I go to town often and there is no reason to expect trouble.'

'Maybe so, but that was before I sent Danton packin','' said Toots. 'He may want to take it out on someone from the Box-B.'

'I'll go with him,' said Sarah. 'They won't dare to do anythin' with me along.'

'Sarah, your speech.'

Sarah looked at her mother's disapproving expression and sighed, her shoulders dropped in resignation. 'Yes, Mother, I meant, 'they wouldn't dare to do anythin'.'

That night, they began a schedule of two men at a time riding four-hour shifts protecting the cattle. During the day, they planned to post a man on the ridge where he could watch both the valley and approaches from town.

Despite Toots' misgivings, Chen and Sarah left early the next morning for Charlo; Chen drove the wagon and Sarah on her pony.

'They're right-smack in the middle, and I need that valley and its water for my cattle.' Griffin paced his office. He stopped to tame his unruly eyebrows – something he often did when he was frustrated. Then, he smoothed his carefully combed gunmetal-grey hair. 'Without it, I can't increase my holdings.'

Danton seated in a chair out of his path, asked, 'Why don't I take care of 'em the way I did the old man and his boy.'

Griffin halted and turned his cold blue eyes to glare at Danton. It was a stare few people experienced and lived to talk about. Without his permission, Danton murdered Baxter and his son, and left their bodies on the open range.

The daughter found them and somehow managed to bring them into town. Though he was careful to cultivate the image of an amiable businessman to the folks in town, the trouble she whipped up among the people of Charlo nearly destroyed Griffin's plans.

'Danton, you pull another stunt like that and I'll have your hide. These people will tolerate a lot, but not blatant murder.'

'I can take care of anyone who makes a fuss,' said Danton.

Griffin leaned down and sneered. 'Like you did that drifter that's now workin' for 'em?'

Danton visibly jerked as if Griffin had slapped him. His hard eyes darkened and his jaw clenched, flexing the muscles in his neck. 'I told you, he got the drop on us from ambush. I'll take care of 'im personal when he pops his head up from that gopher hole they call a ranch.'

Griffin shook his head. 'You're an idiot. I just said we can't afford that kind of trouble.'

'I'll make it look legit. He has to come to town sometime.'

'I meant what I said about your hide,' said Griffin. 'Don't muck things up – now get out of here.'

After he left Griffin's office, Danton headed for the Broken Spoke saloon. Griffin owned it, but A.H. Page fronted it, so the town's folk wouldn't know. Across the street from the saloon's entrance was Murphy's General Mercantile, where he saw Sarah Baxter walk into the store, followed by her Chinaman.

Through the batwing doors of the saloon, he spotted two of his men, Crazy Bill and Hank Springer. They looked up, and he motioned for them to come outside. The three crossed the street to wait for Sarah and Chen to come out of the store.

They lounged on barrels and crates Murphy had staged

on the boardwalk in front of his store. Springer had his hands busy fixing a smoke when Chen and the girl came out carrying packages. So he didn't see Danton trip Chen, who stumbled into Springer knocking his tobacco and paper from his hands.

Chen recovered his footing. He turned to Springer and said, 'Excuse me please.' He stole a look at Danton. 'I seem to be very clumsy today.'

Springer, confused, glanced to Danton, who winked and nodded toward Chen. Understanding flashed in his eyes. He reached out and grabbed the Chinaman. As he swung a roundhouse punch meant to disable Chen, the wiry little man twisted free and ducked. The force of Springer's swing carried him forward stumbling into the street.

Chen, who had not dropped his packages, stepped to the wagon and placed them in the rear behind the seat. Springer gained his feet, and like an angry bull charged at the Chinaman. Again, the spry Chen side-stepped the hulk of a man, and tripped him as he rushed past. Springer crashed into the wooden crates full force and knocked himself unconscious.

Danton and Crazy Bill looked on in amazement. Danton tugged on Bill's shirt and nodded for him to take care of Chen. Bill rose and came down on to the street. Chen remained in the confined isle formed by the wagon and crates. Crouched like an animal aching to pounce, Crazy Bill inched forward.

Arms up guarding his face and body, Bill lashed out with a fierce punch. Chen merely leaned back and the blow missed its mark. As Bill cocked to throw another punch, Chen ducked under Bill's arms and thrust his balled fist into the man's solar plexus. Bill's guard dropped and he bent double gasping for air. Chen stepped in and delivered a chop to the base of Bill's skull; he too was now unconscious.

He looked up at Danton and bowed. In mock pigeon English, he said, 'So solly.'

Danton leapt to his feet and shucked his Colt. As he cocked the hammer, Sarah, who had been watching, slapped his arm as the revolver discharged. The slug meant for Chen's chest slammed into his leg. He flinched, but didn't fall.

Murphy, a stout barrel-shaped bald man, who had come out to see the commotion, grabbed Danton from behind, and held him, while another man took his gun. Danton broke free and turned on the crowd. 'Give me that gun.' Danton jerked it free from the man's hands. He faced Murphy. 'I ought to kill you for that.'

'What goes here?' said a white-haired man in his fifties. His unkempt beard concealed the jowls that hung from his jaw.

'Sheriff,' said Danton. 'The Chinaman attacked my men, and I had to shoot him.' He glared at the men in the crowd. 'Ain't that what happened?'

Murphy said, 'Sheriff Hollister, that's a lie – we're all witnesses. Danton tried to gun down Chen Lee after his men failed to best him in a fight.'

'That's right,' called a man from the crowd, which grumbled its agreement.

Hollister stepped in front of Danton. As he stared at Danton with dull-brown eyes, he worked the ever-present stogy from one side of his mouth to the other. 'Give me your gun, Tom. I got to lock you up until this gets sorted out.'

Danton stepped back and crouched like a cornered cat. 'You come any closer an' I'll plug ya – got that?'

'Danton, surrender your gun to Sheriff Hollister.' The voice was sharp and authoritative; it was Web Griffin, who'd come to investigate why there was shooting. Danton relaxed his stance and let Hollister take his Colt. Griffin stepped in close and whispered. 'If I didn't need you, I'd let you rot in jail. I'll talk to the judge and have you out in the morning. Until then keep your mouth shut and do what Hollister says.'

The sheriff marched Danton toward the jail. Sarah rushed to Chen, who leaned against the wagon for support. 'I'm not badly injured, Sarah, but you'll have to drive the wagon back to the ranch.'

Murphy said, 'Bring him into the store, so we can get him patched up.'

Chen's wound was minor. The bullet passed through the meaty part of Chen's thigh and lodged in a barrel of salt pork staged on the store's boardwalk. An hour later, laying on a makeshift pallet in the rear of the wagon, Sarah and Chen headed for home.

As they drove past the sheriff's office, Sarah saw Web Griffin with Judge Miller. He had his arm across the judge's shoulder and they laughed as they entered the building.

CHAPTER 4

Helen shaded her eyes as she stared across the valley. 'Toots, come quick.'

'What is it, Mrs Baxter?'

She pointed. 'Look there! It's the buckboard, and Sarah's horse is tied behind and she driving. Where's Chen?'

'I'll find out soon enough,' he said and ran to the barn. Knothead waited, saddled for their turn at riding guard on the herd. Toots swung on to his horse and spurred him to a gallop.

He slowed when he saw Chen in the rear and that Sarah appeared unharmed. As he sided the wagon, he stared at Sarah's clenched jaw, her face drawn tight, and her brow scowled.

'What happened, Sarah?' he asked.

'You were right. We oughtn't to have gone. They shot Chen.'

Toots glanced back at Chen, who propped up on his elbow stared back. 'There was no avoiding Danton and his men,' he said. 'Mr Murphy spoke up for us and they put Danton in jail for shooting me.' He rubbed his thigh. 'The wound isn't bad.'

Sarah's voice rose as she spat her words out through

clenched teeth. 'He won't be held for long. I saw Griffin and Judge Miller laughin' it up on their way into the sheriff's office.'

When the wagon drew to a stop at the house, Helen rushed off the porch. Her eyes glistened with concern. 'Sarah!' Then she saw Chen. 'Chen, your leg! You've been hurt.'

'That dirty skunk Danton shot him, Mama.'

Toots watched Helen, but she didn't say a word about Sarah's language. He figured she was too upset about Chen to notice. The men gathered round Sarah wanting to know the details. While Gus and Helen got Chen into the house, Sarah told her story.

'—that polecat Hollister won't keep Danton in jail for long.'

Sarah's account of her story with the addition of a few choice words here and there, unheard by Helen, seemed to release some of her pent-up anger. Toots helped her down from the wagon. Big Nose Karl took the wagon to the kitchen door to be unloaded.

Helen came out on to the porch where Toots and Sarah sat talking. Helen said, 'Chen's wounds aren't serious. The bullet passed through without hitting the bone. I stitched them and put on a tight bandage. He shouldn't be on his feet for a while, but if we can fashion some crutches – he can get around.'

Sarah looked at her mother. 'What are we goin' to do about Danton shootin' Chen? The sheriff and Judge Miller are in Griffin's pocket – they won't stand for the law.'

Helen's eyes narrowed as she stared out at the valley, she was tight-lipped, determined. 'Sarah, they dared to attack you in public. There must be a way to stop them.'

'It's only a three-day ride to Butte. You could send word

to the territorial governor – he'd send someone to investigate.'

Helen's eyes widened; she beamed at Toots with excitement. 'I know Governor Potts, and he is for law-and-order. If I could speak to him, I'm sure he'd start an investigation into Luke's and our son's murder. It would end Griffin's takeover.'

Toots watched as Helen Baxter transformed into a woman possessed. A woman intent on having justice, or was it revenge.

'I'll leave tomorrow,' said Helen.

'Hold on, ma'am,' said Toots, 'you can't just up and run off to Butte without things bein' done first.'

She stared at Toots with hard eyes and set jaw; her fists clenched white at the knuckles. 'Mr McGee, I leave at first light tomorrow morning. Please have everything arranged.'

Toots stood with opened palms, and stared at Sarah with his mouth ajar as if to speak, but nothing came forth. At length, he turned to Helen his shoulder dropped and said, 'Yes, ma'am.'

Helen Baxter drew a deep breath, and smoothed the front of her dress as she exhaled. 'In the morning then.' She made an about-face and marched back into her home.

Sarah, mouth agape, stared after her mother. She blinked her eyes and looked at Toots. 'We can't let her take off to Butte.'

Gus stood by Toots. 'Miss Sarah's got a point. It's too dangerous for Miss Helen to go traipsin' off like that.'

Bewildered, Toots offered only a blank stare.

'Son,' said Gus, 'you said you was the foreman – act like it.'

Gus's tone and words struck home with Toots. 'I don't rightly see how we can stop her from goin', but we can make

43

sure she gets there and back safe enough.'

He surveyed the men. 'Gus, who're the two best shots among the hands?'

Gus pulled off his glove and scratched the thick black stubble on his cheek. 'I reckin that'd be me an' Big Nose Karl – why?'

' 'Cause you, an' him is goin' with Mrs Baxter to Butte.'

Sarah stepped next to Toots and took his arm. 'But, Toots—'

He patted the back of her hand. 'It'll be all right, Sarah. Can your mother ride, I mean like a man?'

'Yes – she and I use to go ridin' when I was – why?'

Toots huddled with Sarah and Gus. 'Here's my plan. . . .'

Helen studied her appearance in the mirror. *From a distance, I might fool someone into thinking I'm a young cowpoke, but not up close.* She was close to fifty, but she retained her woman's figure and was proud of the fact that she could still turn the head of a man, albeit an older one.

Outside at the door from the kitchen, Sarah and Toots waited. Toots inspected her disguise. 'Ma'am, just in case someone's usin' glasses, could you smudge some dirt on your face? You need to keep your bandanna knotted up close to your jaw. No disrespect, ma'am, but you're a hand-some woman, and it's provin' harder to hide 'an I thought.'

Helen's stared into Toots' eyes. 'Thank you, Toots. Considering how I look that's quite a compliment.'

'Ma'am, I -I didn't mean – I just. . . .'

Sarah and Helen both grinned. Helen said, 'I understand what you meant, Toots. You were making an honest observa-tion of my appearance and found my attempt to hide my womanhood lacking.'

Red-faced, Toots nodded.

'That is what makes the compliment so endearing. Don't you see?' Helen leaned over and kissed Toots on the cheek.

He staggered back as if punched. 'Ma'am, I sure hope no one's watchin' the house.'

Both the women broke into laughter, again. Toots's furrowed brow and opened-mouth stare brought them near to hysterics.

'My, my,' said Helen with a deep sigh. 'I haven't laughed like that for months. Thank you, Toots.'

'Yes, ma'am.' He shrugged and left to give final instructions to Gus and Big Nose Karl.

When he returned, he found Chen on his new crutches standing in the kitchen door holding Mr Baxter's English manufactured shotgun. 'You should take the Lang with you, Mrs Baxter.' He broke the chamber and passed it to her. He hobbled inside and brought back a leather bag. 'Here are the shells.'

Mounted by then, Helen leaned down to grab the bag. Chen grasped her hand. 'Please be careful, Mrs Baxter, we wouldn't know what to do without you.'

She gave him a reassuring smile. 'I expect to be gone seven to ten days. I'll be as careful as I can – I promise.' He patted the back of her hand before letting go.

They rode three abreast until they reached the trail, where Gus took the lead. Helen reined up to side him on the left. 'If we pushed hard, could we make it to Butte in two days?'

Gus glanced down at Helen. 'Mrs Baxter, it's been a while since you forked a horse. I figure it'll be closer to four days afore we gets there.'

'We shall see, Gus. We shall see.'

The trail was easy riding and the day, though long, had been uneventful. However, Helen recalled Gus's prediction when she try to step down.

Big Nose Karl and Gus were attending to their animals when Gus glanced up at Helen. She appeared rooted to her saddle. Gus removed the tack from his horse and passed its lead to Karl. He stepped over to Helen. 'Ma'am, do you needs my help gettin' off your hoss?'

Nostrils flared, she winced when she leaned back and tears welled. 'I'm afraid more than my pride is hurt, Gus. You were right. It's been too long since I rode a horse.'

Gus's eyes shone with compassion, but the corners of his mouth curled as he stepped to her horse and let her fall into his arms. Her arm around his neck, she seemed weightless. She hadn't been this close to a man since her husband Luke's death. Her body warmed and she fought the urge to stroke his wide strong shoulders. Instead, she stiffened. 'Right here is fine, Gus, thank you.'

He helped her stand and stood by as she took a few tentative steps. Gus said, 'I'll have your saddle off an' then you've a place to sit and take it easy.'

Her smile was genuine and relaxed. 'Thank you, Gus, but I think I really need to walk around for a bit.'

Gus's stare was blank at first, and then he understood. 'Oh,' he said. 'Stays close so's you can holler iffin' somethin' was to happen.'

Helen hobbled forward up the trail. As she walked, the muscles in her legs loosened and her natural stride returned. Relieved, she returned to their camp, where Gus and Karl were preparing salt pork and beans. 'Gentlemen, may I help in any way?'

'No, ma'am, me and Karl's been cookin' grub on the trail for a mighty long time.'

Helen looked around for her saddle and found that they'd rolled out her bedding. The campfire was near a fallen tree, which provided seating where she could sit and watch them finish cooking. Gus handed her a tin cup of coffee. 'Mrs Baxter, I got a bottle of Old Crow in my saddle-bags, a splash in your coffee might help you sleep easier.'

'Ordinarily, I would refrain, but given the soreness of my' – she paused – 'backside, I believe I will have a splash. Make it generous if you please.'

'Yes, ma'am.' He seemed pleased she liked his suggestion.

The next morning, Helen's head as well as her backside ached, but she didn't complain. She had coffee for breakfast; her stoic manner chided Gus and Big Nose Karl into silence for the day's long ride. Later that night they rode into Butte.

Since the silver played out after the Civil War, the once bustling population of Butte, Montana dropped to one-fifth its boomtown size. However, the Valley Lake Hotel remained, and that's where Helen and her escorts went.

The woman at the hotel's counter did a double take when Helen entered with Gus and Karl following like puppies. As she signed the registry, Helen said, 'Two rooms please – a double for my associates.'

'Yes, ma'am,' said the clerk, who gawked at Helen's garb.

The sun through Helen's window was unwelcome. Her bed, though better than sleeping on the ground, didn't provide the comfort of home. It was near 8.30 by the time she changed to the single dress she brought on the trip, and came downstairs. Seated on a settee in the lobby, Gus stood when she reached the landing.

'Mornin', Mrs Baxter, did ya rest?'

Helen put her hand to her chest and gave Gus a warm heart-felt smile. 'I feel much better this morning, Gus, thank you.'

'Ya goin' to see Potts now?'

'I'd like breakfast first. Have you eaten?'

Gus, holding his hat, worked the brim clear around with his hands. 'Me and Karl had breakfast hours ago, ma'am.'

Helen fought her smile and turned away to compose herself. When she turned back, the corner of her lips remained curled. 'I know it's late, Gus, but would you join me for breakfast – you could have a cup of coffee.'

She wouldn't have thought his mouth could spread so wide. 'Yes, ma'am, I reckon I'd be proud too.' He stepped to the lobby door and held it open.

She paused on the walk and scanned the town. When she and Luke were last here, the streets hummed with activity. When they discovered silver, Butte, Montana sprang into being, literally overnight. Now the town seemed tired.

Their breakfast was awkward; Gus felt ill at ease with the situation, and Helen was preoccupied with Benjamin Potts. She wondered, *would he even remember me after all these years?*

'Mrs Baxter?'

Helen started and looked at Gus. 'Oh, I must apologize, Gus. I'm afraid my mind was on my meeting with the governor.'

'I unnerstan', ma'am. It's close to 10.00. Iffin' you spect t'git in to see 'im we ought to be movin' along.'

At the governor's office the clerk asked, 'Name?'

Helen said, Mrs Helen Baxter. No wait! Tell Benjamin it's Helen Evans-Baxter, an old friend from Ohio.'

The clerk, a small man with thinning hair pasted to his scalp peered over his spectacles with wary eyes and a raised brow. 'Please take a chair with the others, and I'll tell him you're here.' With short quick steps, the clerk darted through the office door like a mouse scurrying to its hole.

Gus, who had stood back, studied Helen with curious

eyes. 'You knows Governor Potts, Mrs Baxter?'

'Once knew, Gus. We're both from Ohio. I met him before I married Luke, and came out here.'

'Oh,' said the big man as he rubbed the front of his shirt and offered a stiff smile.

'The Governor will see you Mrs Evans-Baxter.'

The other people who'd arrived earlier and waited longer stared at her, very much disapproving of her special treatment.

She crossed the room to the door held by the clerk and paused at the doorway. With open windows on two walls, his office was bright and the breeze made it comfortable. As she expected from the outer room, his office was paneled with rich mahogany floor to ceiling, the furniture elegant and, she noted, expensive.

The governor rose and walked around his desk. He'd retained his fit military bearing, but he was thicker than she'd remembered. His hair parted on the side was thinner, and he now sported a full beard that was more salt than pepper.

'Helen, you haven't changed one bit.'

Humor lit her smiling eyes. 'Ever the politician, Benjamin.'

'How can you be so cruel? I only speak the truth,' he said.

They both laughed, as he grasped her hands into his and led her to a chair. When she sat, he took the chair across from her. 'This is a pleasant surprise. I'm sorry to say that I lost track of you after you left Ohio. You're married?'

'I'm a widow, Benjamin, that's partly why I've come.'

'I'm so sorry to hear about your loss, Helen. What can I do to help?'

CHAPTER 5

'Danton, you're a fool,' said Griffin. 'You're lucky that Chinaman was only wounded.'

'But—'

'But nothing. You're goin' to spend a few days in jail for disturbin' the peace.'

'What?'

'You heard me. The townsfolk are touchy since you killed Baxter and his boy. They expect law and order, so the judge sentenced you to five days in jail for disturbin' the peace.'

'Boss, I was only—'

'Would you rather have a trial for attempted murder?'

Danton didn't respond. He dropped on his bunk and rubbed his face. 'OK, I understand, Boss. I'll be more careful.'

Griffin smiled. 'Now you're startin' to understand.'

'Yes, Boss. I won't do anythin' without you sayin' so.'

'Good. I'll make sure your grub is from the café, but no whiskey. When you get out, I need your mind sharp. Got that?'

When Helen finished her story, the governor sat quiet for a long spell before speaking. 'Helen, Web Griffin is an important man in this territory, and he knows many influential

50

people back East. I'm afraid—'

Her nostrils flared as she inhaled. 'Benjamin,' said Helen, her tone very controlled, 'are you telling me that you will not help my family or the people of Charlo?'

Potts's eyes widened and he raised his palms at Helen's bold challenge. 'Helen, I merely wanted to explain that anything to do with Griffin has to be handled carefully, that's all.'

Helen shook her head and gave a long sigh. 'I apologize, Benjamin. Since the death of my husband and son, I've had to deal with trying to keep the ranch and protect my one remaining child, Sarah. I'm afraid it's made me a bit shrewish.'

The governor's manner changed; his tone became soothing. 'Helen, please, there's no need for apologies. I understand your situation. It's just that I need to tread cautiously.'

Her head snapped to look at him. The glare in her eyes spoke louder than her voice. 'You aren't going to help us, are you!'

'Now, now, Helen, I haven't said that. I promise I'll make some inquiries and if need be send someone up to Charlo to look into your claims.'

'My claims.' She stood, placed her hands on the edge of his desk, and leaned forward. 'You don't believe me?'

He reared back and once again raised his hands. 'Helen, please be reasonable. You said yourself there was no proof of your allegations and it's been a long time. People change.'

Helen stood erect and lowered her chin to look at him with cold eyes. 'They certainly do.' She turned and marched from his office, through the lobby and outdoors.

Gus jumped up as she passed and followed her out. 'Is everythin' all right, Mrs Baxter?'

51

'No it's not,' said Helen. Tears welled, but she refused to cry. 'He's turned into a petty politician and doesn't or won't believe my story.'

Gus's face grew red. 'Damn polecat, why I ought to go back in there and whoop his—'

Helen grinned and put her hand on Gus's arm. 'That would land you in jail and leave only Karl to see me home.'

Her words sobered his thinking. 'Yes, ma'am. Speakin' of which, we ought to git to the hotel and gather our possibles.'

Dejected, they collected their belongings and an hour later rode out of town northward towards the Box-B. Helen's somber spirit wore on Gus and Karl, their faces sullen and little exchange of words.

At their evening camp, Helen noticed their behavior. 'Gus, why are you two so glum?'

The men shared glances and it was Gus who spoke. 'Mrs Baxter, it's painful to see you so worried 'bout the Box-B an' all. Me and Karl wants ya to know that we ain't gonna up an' leave ya unprotected. We'll fight. We're scrappers too. Why, down in Texas we seen and done a thin' or two.'

Helen smiled. Their profession of loyalty touched her heart. 'Thank you, Gus. Thank you, both of you. Your promises mean more to me than you'll ever know.'

Karl looked down at his feet, and Gus blushed. 'We jist wanted ya to know, ma'am.'

'You've made me feel better. I think I can go to sleep now. I'll see you in the morning.'

As she walked to her bed-roll, the seed of a thought began to germinate in her mind.

It was the afternoon of the fifth day. Hollister stood in his office with Danton. He said, 'Tom, here's your iron, but

52

mind what Mr Griffin said. Keep it holstered unless he says so.'

Danton slung the rig from his shoulder. With cold eyes, he looked the sheriff up and down. Hollister's gut spilled over his belt. Danton couldn't recall seeing the sheriff on a horse.

'Hollister, you tub of lard, I don't want to see or listen to you for a while, so you'd best stay clear of me.'

The sheriff's face reddened, his jowls jiggled as his lips gaped for words. 'Why you, pup – I ought to knock the hell—'

Danton sneered. 'That'll be the day, fat man.' He turned his back to Hollister, and walked out headed for the saloon.

He pushed through the swinging doors of the Broken Spoke and swaggered to the mahogany bar that ran the length of the room. On the wall behind the bar, over the mirrors were French paintings of women in varies stages of undress and repose.

'Page, get a bottle of Griffin's whiskey. Put it on his tab.'

The saloon owner lifted his bushy eyebrows and looked at Danton, but didn't speak. Danton laid his rig on the bar, placed his hand on the butt of his Colt, and pointed the business end toward Page. The meaning was clear, and the bartender used his bar towel to wipe his balding pate. 'No need, I'll buy,' said Page with a dry chuckle. 'It'll be a get-out-of-jail gift.'

Danton didn't laugh at Page's attempt at humor. Hank Springer and Crazy Bill sat at a table in the far corner of the saloon near the roulette wheel. 'Hey, Tom,' said Springer. 'Hollister gave ya a parole did he?'

He stiffened, then dragged his gun-belt off the bar and strapped it on. Danton tied the holster to his leg when he meant business. He turned to face Springer and Bill. 'The way I see it, it's your fault I had to spent time in jail.'

Springer raised his palms. 'Whoa there, Tom. It weren't our fault, how was we to know that Chinaman was so slick? Iffin' the little bastard would've stood still, we'd of whooped 'im sure.'

'Damn straight,' added Crazy Bill.

Danton relaxed his stance. *Maybe, they want to settle the score with that Chinaman same as me.* He dragged the whiskey bottle off the bar and walked to their table. He dropped into a chair, poured a drink, knocked it back, and sneered at them. 'You boys wanta get even?'

Hank leaned in. 'What ya got in mind, Tom?'

Danton looked at Bill. 'Well, you in or out?'

Crazy Bill angled toward Danton. 'I reckon I'm in.'

Danton glanced over his shoulder to make sure no one was listening. 'I figure we give 'im another week or so for his leg to mend. When things have settled, we gits out to the Box-B and snatch 'im.'

'Then what?' asked Hank.

'We lynch 'im. Leave 'im hangin' from a tree along the trail. I'm bettin' 'em Baxter women will pick up and go then.'

Helen awoke before Gus and Karl. She lay quiet, lost in thought. Sleep had congealed her ideal into a plan of action. Griffin didn't give her any other choice; she had to kill him before he murdered her and Sarah.

She needed help, but she feared that her conscience would not allow her to use Gus as her weapon. As she thought it through, she decided she had no other choice.

'Ma'am, want some coffee?' asked Gus.

'Huh?' She opened her eyes and saw Gus seated on his haunches offering a cup; steam wafted from the liquid's surface. With a smile, she said, 'That would be delightful, Gus.'

Just after dark, they rode down into their valley. Little Mose met them part way to the house. 'There an' back in jist five days,' he said, 'that's some purdy hard ridin'. How ya holdin' up, ma'am?'

'I've become well aware of my age, Mose. It's hard to imagine that I used to ride a horse for pleasure.'

'You showed a lot of sand, Mrs Baxter. Me an' Karl ain't feelin' so spry neither.'

'That's very kind of you to say, Gus, but we both know you and Karl have practically carried me there and back.'

When they reached the house, they rode around to the kitchen door. Through the window, she could see Sarah, Chen, and Toots at the table drinking coffee.

Toots was the first to hear them. He rose and came to the door, followed by Sarah. 'Mother, you're back.' Her tone carried a pleasant surprise.

Chen pushed up from the table when he heard Sarah's greeting. He reached the door in time to see Helen slide from her saddle into Gus's arms. She didn't linger in his arms, but she left a hand pressed against his chest.

Chen stared; she was thankful it was dark as she felt a blush rise in her cheeks. She turned to Gus. 'Thank you, Gus. Without your strong arms to help, I would have to fall off to get down.'

'I was right pleased, Mrs Baxter. Ya kin depend on me.'

After a subtle pat to his chest, she pulled her hand away. 'Thank you, Gus. I'll remember that.'

Gus grinned. He and Karl led the animals toward the barn. Inside the house, Helen nearly collapsed from exhaustion. Sarah helped her to a chair, while Chen prepared food and drink.

Helen looked up. 'Just coffee, Chen. I'm too tired to eat.'

'Nonsense, Mother. You've got to eat something.'

Toots added, 'She's right, Mrs Baxter. A bit of food in your belly an' you'll be spry as a filly tomorrow.'

Helen looked at him; her blue-grey eyes twinkled and the corners of her mouth curled. 'There you go giving me compliments again. Are you flirting with me, Toots?'

Toots' face turned beet red. 'No, ma'am. Why I—'

Sarah burst into laughter, followed by Chen and Helen.

'Aw hell,' he said and stomped out, headed for the bunkhouse.

'You'd better go after him, Sarah,' said Helen, 'tell him I apologize for the teasing.'

Sarah hurried out the door after Toots.

Chen, now seated and sipping coffee, stared openly at Helen.

'What?' she asked, but he didn't respond. She cast her eye downward. 'It's not what you think.'

'I wouldn't be so sure about that, Mrs Baxter. I may know you better than you think.'

Helen leaned back and crossed her arms. She confronted his stare. 'Is that so, Mr Lee?'

'I know that you loved Mr Baxter very much, and it's too soon for anyone else. I know that you are encouraging Mr Wallace, which I suspect is for nefarious reasons. I also know that if you go through with whatever you're planning, you'll regret it for the rest of your life.'

With each word he spoke, Helen's defensiveness dissolved. Her eyes welled, but no tears flowed. 'I've got to do something. Griffin attacked you and Sarah in front of the whole town.'

'It was Danton – and I do not believe Mr Griffin ordered it done. He's not that stupid.'

'How is that supposed to make me feel any better? We're on our own. Potts isn't going to help us.'

'Mother, what are you talking about?'

Helen's attention snapped to the door. Sarah and Toots had returned. How much had they overheard? 'I spoke with Governor Potts. It seems Mr Griffin is an influential man.'

'But, Mama, what're we gonna do?'

'Oh, Sarah, your speech!'

'The devil with my speech. What're we goin' to do if the governor ain't goin' to help us?'

'You've two choices,' said Toots. 'Fight, or cut an' run.'

Helen massaged her forehead then smoothed her hair. She exhaled a long breath. 'This is our home. My husband and son are buried on the knoll above the lake. I can't leave.'

'Then we fight,' said Toots.

Sarah stood next to Toots, her arms held his. 'We fight.'

Helen looked to Chen. His thin lips and clenched jaw conveyed his answer; he merely nodded.

'Where do we begin?' asked Helen. 'We are so few, and Griffin has the money to hire gunmen.'

'I believe the town's with us,' said Sarah. 'Murphy and the others stopped Danton from killin' Chen.'

Toots hadn't heard their conversation. He'd been deciding the next course of action. 'We take the fight to Griffin.'

Sarah stared at him. 'How you figure on doin' that?'

'Sarah, please,' Helen grimaced, 'your speech.'

Toots smiled as Sarah gave an exaggerated sigh. 'Yes, Mother. Toots, please explain how you plan to accomplish that deed?'

'I need to ruminate on that a bit, but it's sure that we can't wait to fight them here.'

'May I suggest,' offered Chen, 'that we all get a good

57

night's sleep before plans are made.'

Toots walked with Chen to the bunkhouse. Chen said, 'You and Sarah make a good couple.'

In the dark, Toots blushed. 'What? Why, all of my talkin' with her has been about her family, you, or the Box-B.'

'Surely you've noticed how she acts when you're present.'

'Chen, she's acted the same since we met – aside from shootin' at me, that is.'

Toots heard quiet laughter coming from Chen. 'Trust me, Toots. We're all aware of how you two act differently when the other is near. One of you has to be the first to say something.'

They reached the bunkhouse before he could respond, so he left the issue hanging, but he wondered if Chen knew what he was talkin' about. *Shucks, even if I wanted to say somethin', I can't till this business with Griffin is settled.* He forced his mind back to the matter of Griffin and the ranch. *Short of outright killin' the bastard, what else can I do?*

CHAPTER 6

Hank Springer, Crazy Bill, and Danton lay along the ridge watching the valley below. 'I ain't got no glasses,' said Springer, 'but that rider down there ain't got red-hair. He must be a new hand. We run off all the others.'

'It don't make no difference,' said Danton in no mood for talk. 'We'll go around the lake. When the Chinaman shows his self we'll grab him, real quiet like.' He took a swig of hooch.

Springer and Bill exchanged glances. Springer said, 'Maybe you ought to take it easy with that bottle, Tom.'

Danton squinted at Springer. 'You think I'm drunk?' Springer gave no response. 'How about you makin' a run for your hoss. I'll count ten before I shoot.'

Springer put his hands up. 'Now, Tom, there ain't no need for you to get mean. We all want the Chinaman, but if you get too deep into that bottle, he might get away – that's all.'

Danton stared at Springer and then turned to Crazy Bill. 'Maybe you're right.' He pushed the cork back into the bottle.

It took two hours for them to skirt the lake to a position where they could watch the ranch's activities. Toward evening, they saw the Chinaman at the rear of the house. On a single crutch, he limped to the hen house with a basket for eggs.

'Now's our chance,' said Danton.

They made their way to behind the barn. 'When he comes back, we rush him. No messin' about this time – got that?' They nodded.

The crutch in one hand and the basket in the other, Chen pushed open the door and started for the house. His basket full of eggs held his attention, so he didn't see or hear them.

Chen became aware of a presence, at the same instant a filthy hand darted from the rear and covered his mouth. An arm encircled his body, pinned his arms, and lifted him from the ground. Someone kicked his crutch away and knocked the basket full of eggs from his hand. When he looked up, he saw Tom Danton's sneering face. Danton drew his revolver and swung it.

When Chen regained consciousness, he remained still and did not open his eyes. His senses informed him; they had him gagged and bound hand and foot. He was no longer at the ranch. The sound of water and the smell of pine tree suggested he was in the forest near the lake – too far away to be heard.

He risked opening his eyes; it was nearly full dark. One of the men neared; he shut his eyes and slowed his breathing.

'You clubbed him too hard, he's still out cold,' he said.

'Bill, get some water and toss it on 'im. That'll wake the little bastard.' Chen recognized Danton's voice.

Chen opened his eyes and moved. 'Aw, he was playin' possum,' said the man called Springer.

The one named Bill laid back and swigged his whiskey.

Unsteady, Danton rose and lurched to Chen. 'Remove

the gag.'

'He'll yell,' said Springer.

'Who cares? Ain't no one out here to hear, but us.'

Springer removed the gag. Chen said nothing. He stared straight ahead not making eye contact with either man.

Danton dropped to one knee and sneered into Chen's face.

'You ain't so slippery now are you?' asked Danton.

Chen ignored Danton. He repeated Confucius's words in his mind: *Silence is a true friend who never betrays. They may kill me, but they will never see my fear or hear me beg.*

Danton slapped Chen across the face splitting his lip. Chen's eyes glistened with the pain, but no tears formed. 'Stand him up, damn it, I'll make the son-of-a-bitch talk.'

Crazy Bill and Hank Springer brought Chen to his feet. Each held an arm, as Danton delivered several blows to Chen's body. He felt his ribs crack; at last, he passed out.

The cold air shocked him back to consciousness; he gasped, but the pain he felt at his ribs caused him to moan involuntarily. He clenched his jaw to stifle the agony. Chen was back on the ground. He glanced toward the men who sat by a small fire drinking whiskey. They hadn't heard him, his lips curled.

'He's a tough little bastard,' said Springer, 'you got to give 'im that.'

'Yeah,' agreed Bill.

'Well, it don't make no difference,' said Danton. 'We'll lynch him soon as he's awake. I want 'im to know it's comin'.'

Outside the bunkhouse, Toots sat with Gus, who had just lit his cigarette. Toots glanced at the house and saw the lamps were still burning in the kitchen. 'Chen must be workin' late – think I'll mosey over to get a cup of Arbuckle's.'

At the kitchen door, Toots peered through to the kitchen. Chen wasn't there, so he walked around to the front of the house; it was dark. Where the hell was Chen at this hour?

Toots swung back to bunkhouse. 'Gus, Chen's not in the house. When's the last time you saw 'im?'

'Let me see,' said Gus as he scratched the stubble on his cheek. 'It was when he went to gather eggs from the hen house.'

'Come on,' said Toots and he turned and darted for the hen house. He stopped when he kicked the egg basket. 'Gus, jingle your spur to the bunkhouse and get a lamp.'

Gus returned with a lamp and the other hands. Toots took the lamp and held it high. By the basket were the broken eggs. Marks in the dirt suggested a struggle.

'They've got Chen,' said Toots. 'Stay away from this area 'til we get enough light to see.'

The kitchen door slammed and they all turned and stared.

'What's going on out here?' asked Helen, pulling her robe tight to cover her gown.

All but Toots looked away. 'It appears Chen is missin'.'

'When?' she asked.

'We're not sure,' said Toots. 'Gus saw him goin' to the hen house just before dark, so my guess is four or five hours.'

'Let's start looking for him.'

'Mrs Baxter, hold on a minute,' said Toots. 'We can't see anythin' without light so we'd just be wastin' time, and maybe settin' the rest of us up for an ambush.'

Helen's white-knuckled fists twisted her robe's tie.

Toots turned and counted heads: Gus, both Moses, and Big Nose Karl were here. Pete's tendin' the herd?'

Karl nodded. 'He relieved me over an hour ago.'

'So you didn't see or hear anythin'?' asked Toots.

'Nope. Just cows.'

'Maybe they're still close by,' said Toots. 'Little Mose, I want you to ride out and tell Pete what's goin' on and to keep an eye out for anythin' suspicious. Then ride up to the ridge and make a couple of passes lookin' for anythin' out of the ordinary. If you see anything fire two shots – got it?'

Chen stole a glance. Danton, Springer, and Bill had consumed their whiskey. They sat, each in a drunken stupor. If Chen was ever to escape, now was his chance. They'd used leather straps to tie his hands and feet, which were damp with blood and sweat.

He took a slow breath and held it. He hoped to minimize the pain from his broken ribs. His lungs inflated, he worked his wrist to stretch the leather. Finally, he freed his hands. Bending to reach his feet caused excruciating pain.

Danton grunted and looked his way. Chen froze hoping that he was too drunk to see; his luck held. Danton slumped over on his side and passed out.

Free, Chen got to his hands and knees and crawled among the trees and bushes away from their camp. He was too hurt to ride, so finding their horses was moot. To survive, he had to stay hidden until the Box-B noticed him missing.

It seemed like hours but he found a small outcrop fronted with thick bushes. It was painful to work his way between them, but his adrenaline masked the pain enough to succeed.

At some point after he lay quiet for a while, he drifted off into a deep sleep. The sound of voices woke him.

'Where'd the little sum-bitch get to?' It sounded like Springer. 'He couldn't have gone far busted up the way he was.'

Chen must have slept for hours. It was still dark, but Danton and his men were close to being sober, which required hours of sleep. Each man had a candle and stomped around through the trees searching for Chen.

'It'll be daylight soon,' said Bill. 'Maybe we ought to ride out of here while we still can.'

Danton snarled. 'I mean to string up that little bastard, and we don't leave before then. Now keep your eyes on the ground and look for signs. He ain't no damn Injun, there must be somethin'.'

They stumbled closer to his location. He thought about what they said. *Did I leave a trail to where I'm hiding?* He strained to see but it was too dark.

Two shots rang out loud and clear. After an extended pause, there were two more rounds fired followed by a single crack from a rifle a long way off.

'Damn, Tom, it's a signal,' said Springer. 'They've seen our candles.' He blew his out and turned toward their camp.

'Where do you think you're goin'?' asked Danton.

'Tom, they'll be on us soon enough,' said Springer, 'let's get while we still can.'

Danton yanked his Colt and pointed it at Springer's gut. 'You try to leave before I say and I'll kill you. Now keep lookin'.'

Springer glanced at Crazy Bill, who shrugged and continued his search for Chen. 'Tom, you're goin' to get us all killed – can't you see that?'

'I'm warnin' you for the last time. Not another word.'

Springer struck a match and relit his candle.

Horses saddled, the Box-B men waited for dawn to follow Chen's trail, when Little Mose fired the shots. Karl and Gus each had a lantern, so they led. Toots and Big Mose trailed.

Little Mose ground-reined his mount, fished a candle from his saddle-bags, and lit it. He passed it back and forth to signal his location to the oncoming riders.

Within minutes, they arrived. 'What'd you see?' asked Gus, holding up his lantern to see Little Mose better.

Mose gazed at the stars. Soon, he fixed on one and then pointed. 'I saw lights flickerin' in that direction. It looked like candles, but I'm not so sure now.'

'Lower your lantern, Gus. You too, Karl,' said Toots as he rode forward into the darkness on the ridge. He waited for several seconds for his eyes to adjust. As his pupils opened and he could make out the tree line, he saw the lights. *Three lights moving through the trees, what did they mean?*

Then it came to him. 'Chen's escaped and they're searching for him. Gus, Karl pass your lanterns and grab your rifles.'

They passed off the lanterns and rode to Toots, who had dismounted. 'What are you thinkin', Toots?'

Toots levered a round into his long gun. 'I aim to fire on them lights and hopefully scare them away from Chen.'

'What about Chen?' asked Gus. 'You might hit him?'

'Can you make out the tree line?' Gus and Karl nodded. 'Shoot into the tree tops. The rounds whizzin' by should be enough.'

They fire off several rounds, but the candles remained lit. Gus said, 'It ain't workin'.'

'OK,' said Toots, 'start lowerin' your shots. We'll know when to stop.'

After, a few volleys, each lower than the previous, the candles blinked out. 'Hold your fire,' said Toots. 'We'll ride down there at first light.

Less than an hour later, the sun warmed their backs and they waited for it to crest the ridge and flood the forest below with light. Toots had laid his rifle on the ground pointing in the direction they'd been shooting.

When the sun cleared the ridge, he picked out a landmark, mounted and rode down the slope into the pines. They rode slowly through the trees calling Chen's name. It was a full hour's search before they heard a feeble, 'Here, I'm here.'

They had to use their lariats to pull the bushes away to reach Chen. Toots was shocked to see how badly he'd been beaten. When he tried to help Chen to his feet, Chen pushed away his hand. 'My ribs are broken and I'm bruised up inside. I can stand, but I can't walk far or ride a horse.'

With their bed-rolls, they constructed a litter and carried Chen back to the trail, where a wagon waited. 'Pete, drive real slow and careful back to the house. Karl, you ain't known in town, so I want you to go fetch the doctor. Use force if you have to, but get him out here first thing.'

Karl nodded, reined his pony for Charlo, and spurred him to a gallop.

'Big Mose, Little Mose, you two and Pete hole up inside the house. I don't expect Griffin ordered this, but just in case I want you to be ready.'

Pete started the wagon toward the house with Big and Little Moses one on each side.

'Gus, if you're up for it, we've got business in town.'

'Just been waitin' for you to ask.'

CHAPTER 7

The bullets buzzed the treetops like angry bees. Springer and Bill looked to Tom. He said, 'They're bluffin'. They won't shoot lower or they'd risk hittin' their Chinaman. Keep lookin'.'

The third fusillade dropped down below the treetops, the fourth even lower. Finally, Danton regained his senses and snuffed out his candle. 'Come on. We're gettin' out of here.' He made for his horse; Springer and Bill were close on his heels.

People were up and about when they rode into Charlo. Danton was completely sober and his head throbbed. His first stop was the saloon, which wasn't yet open. Page turned as Danton entered, walked behind the bar, and poured a beer. 'It's early even for you, Tom.'

'Hair of the dog.' He tilted his head back and poured the foamy liquid down his throat. 'Aah. I think I'll live.' He poured a second and drank it at an unhurried pace. 'Seen Griffin?'

'If he's up, I expect he's at the hotel havin' breakfast.'

Danton finished his beer, nodded, and let himself out the way he came in. He expected trouble from the Box-B, and if he wanted to keep his hide, he had to tell Griffin.

Danton stalled at the door to the restaurant. Eventually, he saw Griffin at a table in the rear behind a waiter who poured him coffee. He waited for Griffin to look up and see him before he walked across the room.

When he sat down, Griffin said, 'Tom, you smell like bad booze and horses. When's the last time you had a bath?'

'Never mind that, Mr Griffin.'

Griffin shot him a sharp look. 'What've you done now?'

Danton's eyes darted about the restaurant; no one paid them any attention. He leaned forward and in a low tone, he said, 'Me and a couple of the boys went out to the Baxter place.'

'Damn it, Tom. What'd you do?'

'Well, we figured if they found their Chinaman lynched. . . .'

The blood drained from Griffin's face as he bolted upright and stared at Danton, his words a whisper. 'You lynched Lee?'

'Nah, we just roughed him up some, but the ranch hands didn't take it well and they're after us.'

Color returned to Griffin's face, and he leaned toward Danton. 'I told you to stay away from them and not to do anything, unless I ordered.' His head bowed; he shook it, and with a sigh, he looked back up at Danton. 'I should let them take you, but that would cause problems. Meet me at my office in fifteen minutes. I'll give you some money, so you and the men who helped you can get of town.' He paused. 'Don't come back.'

Griffin stood and walked away from the table, paying the waiter on the way out.

Danton was stunned. *How could Griffin just abandon me like this? After all the thing's I did for 'im that he wouldn't do his self.*

Why I ought to. . . .

Danton walked into Griffin's office; the safe was open. 'Here's $2,000. Leave town and never return. Is that clear?'

Danton nodded, but he didn't take the offered money. 'Griffin, I did a lot of dirty work for you and this is all I get?'

He tossed the money on his desk and brought his right hand from behind his back; he cocked the revolver. 'It's your choice, Tom,' Griffin sneered. 'Take the money and leave, or I'll shoot you for attempted robbery. That won't be hard to sell after the town finds out about Lee. Hell, I might even get a medal.'

Deep furrows ran across Danton's brow and his eyes stared hard at Griffin. 'You'll pay for this double cross, Griffin.'

'Tell me again why I shouldn't plug you right now,' asked Griffin and he raised the revolver.

Danton reached slowly and picked up the money. 'All right, I'm leaving.' He backed his way out of Griffin's office.

He found Springer and Crazy Bill at the saloon. Both were eating beans and beef and washing it down with beer. Danton motioned to Page to provide him the same.

'How'd it go with Griffin?' asked Springer.

'The bastard's throwin' us over. We gotta get out of town.'

The town and its haunts were unknown to Toots. 'Where's this Griffin hang his hat durin' the day, Gus?' asked Toots.

Gus looked around. 'He's got an office, other end of town.'

Toots nodded and Gus led off. They stopped in front of a single story brick building of shotgun style design. Painted on the window was 'W. Griffin—Land and Cattle Investments.'

They stepped down together. Toots said, 'Shuck your long

gun and stay out here. Any trouble, I'll come a-runnin'.'

Gus nodded and moved to stand with his back against the brick wall. 'Just let 'em sons-a-bitches try somethin'. I'll shove lead up their asses.'

Toots chuckled at the comment and walked into the office. The anteroom was smallish, but with fancy decorations. It reminded him of the hotel lobby in Denver. At the single desk sat a spindly man who wore sleeve protectors and a visor. The visor ringed the man's baldness.

'Can I help you?' he asked.

Toots laid his Winchester in the crook of his left arm and faced the clerk. 'I'm lookin' for Griffin.'

The clerk swallowed hard. 'D-do you have an appointment?'

Toots pulled back the hammer on his rifle. The clerk's eyes widened. 'Who shall I say is calling?'

A noise came from the inner office. Toots took several long steps and burst through the half-opened door, his rifle leveled at Griffin.

Griffin was half out of his chair with his hand inside a desk drawer. Toots said, 'Show me your hands. They'd better be empty, or you'll eat what's in 'em.'

The muffled clunk of a gun as it fell back into the drawer drifted across the room and Griffin stood erect and raised his empty hands. With his rifle, Toots waved for Griffin to come from behind his desk. As he complied, Toots instructed him to sit in one of the two leather chairs stationed in front of his desk.

'What's this about, young man?'

Toots smiled. 'The easy way would be to just plug ya and leave town. I doubt anyone would miss you, or the way you do business.'

'Why I'm a pillar of this community, and I'll—'

'Shut up,' said Toots. Griffin's face began to flush with anger. 'Now like I was sayin', there's the easy way, but I'd have to leave town. I like it here. What I mean to say is I like it at the Box-B.'

Griffin emotions subsided and his face regained its usual color. 'What is this all about?'

Toots' eyes narrowed and his jaw clenched. 'It's about you killin' Baxter and his son. It's about you sending Danton out to lynch Chen Lee.'

Griffin put his hands in the air. 'I had nothing to do with either of those acts.'

'You denyin' Tom Danton works for you?'

'He did, but not any longer.' Griffin's thin lips curled and his eyes twinkled with confidence.

'That so?' asked Toots.

As he nodded, Griffin couldn't refrain from grinning. 'Paid him off a couple hours ago and told him to leave town. I don't need the kind of trouble he causes.'

Toots stepped forward and slammed the rifle's barrel across Griffin's right ear splitting the tissue and raising a knot. Griffin slumped in his chair holding the side of his head.

'Why'd you do that?'

'I just couldn't abide your possum grin.' He paused to let Griffin regain his composure. 'Now you listen to me. You're done in Charlo, the county – hell, the state of Montana. After I get Danton, I'm comin' back for you.'

A red flush grew on Griffin's face. 'You fool. I've got the law on my side. I'll wire the governor, and the whole state will be after you.'

'That may be, Griffin, but it won't stop me from killin' you. You'd best be gone from these parts before I get back.' With that said, he backed out of Griffin's office, closing the

71

door as he went.

The anteroom was empty. Outside, Gus remained on guard. Toots asked, 'Where'd the clerk get to?'

Gus grinned. 'He lit out of here like his tail was afire headed straight to Hollister's office. Did you get anythin' out of Griffin?'

'Yeah. Danton's lit out and got maybe a two-hour head start. We ain't got time to deal with the sheriff right now. Let's jingle our spurs.' They rode out of town at a gallop.

The fear of an ambush was constant. So, over the next couple of days, they fell into a routine of staying back and trailing their horse prints. The lead rider's horse, they assumed to be Danton, had an odd hoof print. The front right shoe wasn't fitted correctly and was distinctive from its other three.

On the third day, Toots said, 'Gus, I want you to head back to the Box-B and handle things. Mrs Baxter needs your help.'

Gus tilted his head and looked sideways at Toots. 'What're you goin' to do? You can't handle 'em all by yourself.'

Toots grinned at the old-timer. 'There's no need to worry none. I got talents Danton wouldn't begin to understand. My concern is for Sarah and Mrs Baxter. You head on back and take care of them.'

William McGee, before he met Toots's mother was a mountain man, who at varies times lived with Indians. He learned to hunt and track with them in his younger days; his father passed along those skills. Toots was a formidable outdoorsman and tracker. He had Danton's horse's hoof print imprinted on his brain. He'd be able to identify it like a known face in a crowd.

His plan was to dog Danton until he got lazy, felt safe, and let his guard down; he'd take him then.

72

*

Six days later, Danton and his men were near the Wyoming border. They'd made an early camp to rest up.

Toots watched them from the trees upstream of where they camped. They sat on logs dragged to the campsite by an enterprising traveler long ago.

Danton, said, 'I think we're clear, boys. If they were comin' for us, we'd've seen 'em by now. We'll be in Wyoming tomorrow.'

Springer asked, 'What're we goin' to do there, Tom?'

Danton chuckled. 'Hank, you're always the worrier.' Springer's concerned expression didn't relent. 'As long as there're cattle and homesteaders, we've got work. We'll find somethin' soon enough.'

Toots waited until dark before he started making his way toward their camp. He stood in the darkness and watched. Danton brought out a bottle of hooch. 'Want a snort before we turn in?'

Two pulls on the bottle turned into several. They were feeling mellow and off guard when Toots walked into their camp with his Winchester and Colt, ready to bring death.

Springer seemed the most dumbstruck and didn't react. Crazy Bill threw himself to the ground and rolled away from the others. Danton jerked his iron and fired, but too fast, the shot went wild. Toots let go with the Winchester putting a slug in the middle of Danton's chest. He collapsed like a wet rag.

Crazy Bill rose up with his revolver and took aim. Toots lifted his Colt, already cocked, and drilled Bill through his left eye; his head twitched as a piece of his skull blew free.

Springer finally came to life and reached for his cap and

73

ball Navy Colt. Still seated, the hog leg never cleared its holster. Toots put two slugs through his chest. Springer released his revolver and clawed at his clothes as if they were on fire. His confused look became a vacant stare and he tumbled backwards over the log.

Crouched, Toots swung the Colt as he scanned the camp; Danton and his men were all down. His eyes blinked as if returning from a daydream; he stood erect and exhaled a long breath. The cold rage sent a shiver through his body, so he moved closer to the fire to warm himself.

Minutes past, he couldn't be sure; then he heard a moan. He whirled toward the sound; it was Danton, but he didn't move. Toots approached with caution, his revolver's hammer cocked. He stood over Danton.

Danton remained where he fell, his eyes glazed, his skin ashen, and a dark stain spread on his chest. His eyes focused on Toots. 'I can't feel my arms or legs – nothin'. I'm dyin'. Please, I don't want to die.'

'You should've considered how it was goin' to end when you was robbin' and killin'.'

'B-but, I don't want—'

'What you want ain't got nothin' to do with it – you're goin' to meet your maker sure enough. You can set the record straight; it might help some when you meet 'im.'

Danton began to sob. 'I should've done better. I was raised right, but—'

'Damn it, Danton. You're done – take it like a man.'

A bit of color returned to his face, his eyes glared, and his jaw clamped tight. Toots saw a change; Danton's face relaxed and his voice sounded calm.

'OK, I'm same as dead. I ought to make things right.' Danton confessed to Toots everything he knew about Griffin, and his plans for Silverbow County, including about

74

his ambition of becoming governor. When he finished, he asked, 'I could use a drink, anythin' left in that bottle?'

Toots rose and stepped to the fire. There lay the bottle, with just a taste left. He poured it into one of the tin cups and returned to Danton. He raised his head and gave him the drink of hooch.

Danton licked his lips. 'That'll be my last drink of whiskey.' His eyes widened with fear, and then his courage returned. 'You tell Griffin I'll see him in—'

'I expect you will if I have a say in the matter.'

When morning came, Toots buried the three men because it was the right thing to do, but left no marker, or said any words.

Four days later, Toots reined up at the main house of the Roberts' place. Mr Roberts stood by the corral watching one of his men work a roan stud through its paces.

He glanced over his shoulder at Toots. 'Didn't 'spect to see you so soon, son, you come back for that job?'

'No sir, I come to see you.'

'Well, c'mon to the house, there's Arbuckle on the stove.'

They sat at the kitchen table. Toots's mouth began to water from the aroma of fresh-baked bread. Mrs Roberts, a tiny woman with shiny white-hair stared at them with intense blue eyes, eyes that Toots guessed didn't miss much.

Using the tail of her apron to hold the hot pot, she poured them coffee. 'I just took bread from the oven. Like some?'

Toots's face lit up. 'Yes, ma'am.'

She placed the bread on the table along with butter and honey. 'You men cut what you want. I'll leave you to it,' she said, and left them alone so they could talk in private.

'Now then,' said Mr Roberts. 'What'd you come to see me about?'

By way of providing context, Toots told him about Danton's attempted lynching of Chen Lee, his own run in with Griffin, and how he'd hunted down Danton and his men.

'—and before he died, Danton confessed,' said Toots.

'That's some tale, young man.' Roberts studied Toots for a long time. Toots understood how his story might seem a bit on the tall side. The old man's face softened, he smiled, and his blue eyes sparkled with excitement 'I'd of liked to've been there.' After a few seconds, Roberts sobered and asked, 'What'd this Danton fella confess?'

'Well, sir. He admitted to killin' Baxter and his son right enough, plus a few others that stood in Griffin's way. You see Griffin plans. . . .' Several minutes passed, as Toots related all the information he learned. 'He's a mighty ambitious man.'

CHAPTER 8

The clerk came into his office. 'Mr Griffin, you've got a telegram. It's from Governor Potts.'

Griffin took the offered piece of paper and read:

GRIFFIN STOP MRS BAXTER CAME TO SEE ME STOP GRIEV-ING STOP CLAIMS YOU HAD SOMETHING TO DO WITH HUSBAND'S DEATH AND YOU WANT RANCH STOP SHE IS FRIEND FROM OHIO STOP DO WHAT YOU CAN TO HELP HER STOP BENJAMIN POTTS GOVERNOR.

'Damn it,' he said. *I hadn't planned for that. With the governor nosing around, I need to be smarter about this. Why couldn't Baxter agree to sell? It was a fair price.*

The idea came to him like a flash. *Why hadn't I thought of this sooner?* Griffin bolted to his feet. As he passed his clerk, he said. 'I've gone to see Hollister. I'll be back soon.'

Later that day, the sheriff knocked on Griffin's door before entering. 'Hollister, you returned straight away. Good, good.'

Griffin's smile was friendly. 'Come in and sit down.'

Hollister's brow lifted; his smile was fixed and tight-lipped. He worried the documents in his hands. 'I found them.'

'C'mere, let's have a look.'

'Yes, sir,' said Hollister as he stepped toward Griffin's desk and handed him the papers.

Griffin unfolded the documents, deed records for the Baxter ranch. There were numerous samples of Luke Baxter's handwriting and signature, which would serve his purpose well.

'These will do nicely, Hollister. No one saw you take them from the recorder's office?'

'No, sir, I was real careful.'

Griffin took pen and paper from his desk and set to work copying Luke's signature. 'How long's it goin' to take?' asked Hollister.

'Not long – his signature isn't elaborate. I'd say an hour's practice should do it—'

'Ahem,' said Hollister. 'You want me to come back later?'

'Yeah, come back in a couple of hours and then you can return the deed papers to the recorder's office. Don't get caught. Then come back again tomorrow morning around ten and bring Judge Miller with you.' Without waiting for a response, he reverted back to his practice and didn't notice as Hollister left.

At ten o'clock the next morning, Hollister, with Judge Miller in tow, arrived at Griffin's office. The clerk looked up as they entered. 'He's expecting you.'

The door was open and Griffin sat at his desk; he was grinning as he examined a sheet of paper. He glanced at them as they entered. 'Judge, sheriff, please come in. I've been waiting for you.'

Miller and Hollister looked at each other with quizzical expressions. Miller asked, 'What's got you in such a good mood, Web? I can't say I've ever seen you so happy.'

As they seated themselves in front of Griffin's desk, he slid the document he studied over for them to see. 'Judge, I want you to issue an eviction order on the Baxter Ranch.'

The judge's eyes widened and he stared with an open mouth. Griffin nodded toward the paper. Miller fumbled in his pocket and retrieved his glasses.

Miller held out the paper. 'I didn't know you bought their place. Why haven't you said anything before?'

Griffin glanced at Hollister and smiled. 'Baxter sold it to me days before his death. I didn't want to push the issue while his family grieved, but—'

'That's damn nice of you, Web. But why evict 'em? Show 'em this bill-of-sale.'

'I have, Judge. Mrs Baxter claims it's not her husband's signature.'

'Well that ought to be easy enough to prove. There's got to be records with Baxter's signature.'

'I already thought of that. That's why I had the sheriff ask you here. I want you personally to confirm the signature; when you're satisfied that it's bona fide, then issue the eviction papers. Hollister will serve 'em.'

'I'll check the county records now.' Miller stood and looked at Hollister. 'You comin'?'

'Nah, I got business with Mr Griffin.'

They watched the judge leave. Hollister rose and closed the door. 'You really think this will work?'

Griffin grinned like a Cheshire cat. 'How would it not? The only person who can dispute the bill-of-sale is dead.'

Hollister's brow furrowed. 'What about Mrs Baxter?'

'That's why I wanted the judge to verify Baxter's signature. Once he's convinced, there'll be nothing she can do about it.'

'Why didn't you let him in on it?' asked Hollister.

Griffin shook his head. 'He's a federal judge appointed by the president. He's turned a blind eye to some of the minor things I've done, but not this. The Baxter woman knows that, which is why this plan will work. If she goes to the governor again for help, I'll have Judge Miller to back me up.'

Hollister rubbed the back of his neck. 'If the judge don't agree that it's Baxter signature, then what?'

'You should learn to have faith in your fellow man. The judge and the governor want to believe that it's his signature. It's in their best interest for me to be successful.'

Hollister's eyes widened and he smiled. 'Oh, it's greed. You're workin' the money angle.'

Griffin was beginning to feel like a schoolteacher. 'That's part of it, but it's the power and influence that my money provides that's most important to 'em.' He looked at Hollister's expression and saw he was wasting his time. 'It's politics—'

'I get it,' said the sheriff.

Just after the midday meal, Judge Miller returned to Griffin's office. The clerk announced his arrival.

'Show him in,' said Griffin, as he rose to greet Miller.

The judge was not alone; he had Jeff Blevins, the town's prosecuting attorney with him. 'Web, I brought Jeff with me to insure we proceed within the guidelines of the law.'

Griffin stood erect, his eyes pinched at the corners, his mouth turned down. The room was silent for several heartbeats, and then he regained his composure.

With a gracious smile, Griffin stuck out his hand. 'Mr Blevins, it's been a while since we've talked. How are you and your lovely wife?' He added before Blevins could respond. 'You've two children too, as I recall – a boy and girl?'

Blevins returned the smile. 'We're all well, thank you.'

Griffin turned to Miller. 'Please, both of you be seated.' He waited as they found chairs. 'Now tell me, have you confirmed Baxter's signature?'

'Well, Web, there's a problem,' said Miller. 'We believe it's Baxter's signature, but it ain't witnessed.'

'What does that mean?' said Griffin through his clenched teeth. He was on his feet.

'No need to get head up, Mr Griffin,' said Blevins. 'It's just that it's your word against Mrs Baxter, unless of course she accepts the signature as genuine.'

'Why wouldn't she?' said Griffin. 'I reckon she ought to know her husband's signature.'

Blevins pressed on. 'If she contests the signature it's your word against hers. You should have had it witnessed.'

Griffin's mind raced. He grabbed at the first plausible idea that came to him. 'Hollister was here; he saw Baxter sign the bill-of-sale, and me give him the money. Hell, that's probably why he and the boy were killed.'

'Well that's different,' said Miller, 'if Hollister witnessed the signature, and he will sign an affidavit to that affect, I'm sure—'

'You wait right here. I'll get my clerk and you can dictate it to him and while you're doing that I'll go and find Sheriff Hollister.'

Griffin was through the door and returned with his clerk before Miller or Blevins could protest. He instructed the clerk and vanished to find Hollister.

His gold timepiece read nearly 2 p.m.; he knew where to find Hollister. He stormed down the planked walk to the Broken Spoke. Hollister sat watching the faro players and nursing a beer.

The sheriff looked up as Griffin approach. 'C'mere,' said Griffin as he headed to Page's office.

81

Inside the office, Griffin closed the door. 'The judge needs for you to sign an affidavit sayin' you saw Baxter sign the bill-of-sale to his ranch.'

Hollister hid his hands behind his back and stepped away from Griffin. 'I wasn't there, Mr Griffin. I'd be lyin' to the judge and—'

Griffin closed the gap between them and leaned in. 'You listen to me closely, Hollister. If you want to keep your job and stay healthy, then you'll do as I say.'

'—but, Mr Griffin.'

As if by magic, a .45 Derringer appeared in Griffin's hand, and he poked it into Hollister's fat gut. Hollister paled, his mouth moved, but no sound came. Griffin inhaled deeply and stepped back as he blew out the breath. He pocketed the Derringer and forced a smile. 'I can see that I'm goin' about this all wrong.' Griffin reached out and straightened the shcriff's rumpled shirt. 'Let's start over. I need for you to sign that affidavit, and I'll pay you five hundred dollars. What do you say?'

'Let me explain, Mr Griffin.' Griffin nodded. 'If I sign and the judge finds out that it's fake, it'll connect me to the Baxter murders. Don't you see?'

A genuine smile spread across Griffin's face. 'You think I killed the Baxters?'

Hollister's confusion was obvious; finally, he said, 'Well no, but Danton works—'

Without a hint of it's coming, Griffin was riled again. 'I never said anythin' to Danton about murder. If he was the one who killed 'em, he did the deed on his own.'

'But that ain't how they'll see if it's found out.'

'It's your choice. Five hundred dollars or. . . .' Griffin patted the vest pocket with the Derringer.

'I'll sign it, Mr Griffin, but you gotta tell 'em I didn't have nothin' to do with murder if this goes wrong.'

Griffin sighed. 'Sure, I promise. Now here's what to say.'

When Griffin came back to his office, Blevins had left. Judge Miller stood at the clerk's desk chatting when they entered.

'Sorry, Judge. I finally found him at the Spoke.'

The judge glanced at the wall clock. 'It's a bit early, but in any case. . . .' The judge led them into Griffin's office. 'Sheriff, Web tells me you were here to witness the sale of Baxter's ranch. Is that correct?'

Prepared for a lengthy explanation, Hollister seemed surprised when the judge passed him a sheet of paper. 'What's this?' he asked.

'Why it's an affidavit,' said Miller. 'You swear that you witnessed the sale of Baxter's ranch.'

Hollister glanced at Griffin. Griffin patted his vest pocket and grinned, but his smile held no humor.

'Sure,' said the sheriff. 'I'll be happy to sign it.'

There was a slight tremor in Hollister's hand, but only Griffin saw it. Griffin asked, '—the eviction notice, judge?'

'Sheriff, come by my office in a few hours. It'll be ready.'

Miller turned to Griffin. 'Anythin' else I can do for you?'

Griffin exhaled a long breath. 'Well, Judge, I know you said it was a bit early, but I've some very fine brandy and—'

'Say no more, Web. I'm not a prude about such things, it's just – I'm a judge after all and have to set an example. But, there's always an exception. Where's this fine brandy?'

Griffin put his arm around the judge's shoulder. 'Have a seat while I pour us a glass.'

As Griffin entertained the judge, he saw Hollister place the affidavit on his desk, and without a peep, sneak out the door.

*

Hollister hurried through the batwing doors at the Broken Spoke. Page tended the bar. 'Give me a whiskey. Make it a double.' He tossed the hooch down the back of his throat. His face grimaced as it burned, then he felt its warmth radiate from his core. 'Another, Page. You can leave the bottle.'

Page's brow wrinkled and his eyes squinted as he focused his attention on the sheriff. 'What's happened, Hollister? You act like you seen a ghost or somethin'.'

Hollister's chuckle was thick with sarcasm. 'It's somethin' all right, I'm thinkin' about quittin' this town.'

'Calm down, Gil. Have you talked to Griffin? Maybe he can help with whatever's botherin' you.'

The sheriff reached out and grabbed Page's arm and looked about to make sure no one listened. 'Not a word to Griffin, ya hear. He'd kill me for sure.'

'Gil, we're friends. I don't want to see you get into trouble, but tell me what's goin' on here. Maybe I could help.'

Hollister knocked back his third drink. His speech became slurred. 'D-don't say nothin' to G-Griffin. He's the reason I'm g-goin' to leave. Promise you won't say nothin'.'

'Sure, Gil, whatever you say.'

'You're my pal, Page.'

'Listen, Gil, there's a cot in my office. Why don't you go lie down and rest a while. I'll wake you in a couple of hours.'

Hollister stumbled through the bar room to Page's office. Inside, he dropped across the cot and promptly passed out.

A couple of hours later, as promised, Page came into his office with a tray of food and hot strong coffee. He kicked Hollister's boot. 'Wake up, Gil.'

Hollister stirred. 'What—' His eyes darted about the room. Finally, he focused on Page. 'Does Griffin know I'm here?'

'I ain't seen him. Why?'

'Page, forget what I said earlier. I was upset that's all.'

'Sure, Gil, whatever you say.'

The loud ticking of the wall clock behind him attracted his attention. 'What's the time?'

'Nearly five.'

'Oh shit. I'm supposed to be at Judge Miller's by now.' *What kind of trouble have I gotten into? Maybe I should tell the judge the truth, but then Griffin would kill me for sure. I could run, but how far would I get?*

At Miller's door, he paused. Finally, he decided and entered.

'Been waitin' on you, sheriff. Here's the notice. You goin' out there alone?'

CHAPTER 9

Hollister crested the ridge above the Baxter ranch. Scanning the valley, he saw a rider headed his way with his long gun free and its butt propped on the rider's leg. As the rider reined up, he asked, 'Somethin' we kin do fer ya, sheriff?'

'Howdy, Mose,' said Hollister. 'I got some palaverin' to do with Mrs Baxter. It's business.'

Little Mose rode up to the crest and looked past the sheriff to scan the forest. Hollister said, 'I'm alone, Mose.'

'All right, you kin head on down to the main house. You need to know they'll be watchin' you ride in, an' they're armed and ready after what happened to the cook.'

Hollister halted and looked back. 'The cook?'

'Yep, that sum-bitch Danton tried to lynch 'im.'

'I hadn't heard,' said Hollister. He turned back in his saddle and rode away toward the ranch.

Hollister reined his horse at the house. On the porch, Chen Lee reclined on a makeshift pallet. His leg bolstered on a pillow, he looked like he'd survived a cattle stampede, just.

As he started to dismount, he heard the distinctive click of a shotgun; he paused, and then lowered back into his saddle. Hollister glanced at Chen, who pointed the Lang.

'Mr Lee. I'm here on legal business, nothin' more.'

'Apologies, Sheriff, but as you can see, I'm not feeling well, and it makes me irritable. What do you want here?'

'I've come to see Mrs Baxter. Is she about?'

Sarah heard and came to the door. 'What do you want?'

Hollister decided that patience was his best course. 'Sorry, Sarah, but I need to see your mother. Please tell her I'm here.'

Sarah walked away without comment. A few minutes later Helen came out on to the porch. 'I'm sure you'll forgive my poor manners – given the circumstances. What is it that you want?'

The sheriff fumbled around inside his shirt and produced the papers. He sided the porch and handed them to Helen.

She unfolded the papers and read, 'NOTICE OF EVICTION, you have thirty days.'

Her face paled as her arm lowered and the paper dropped to the porch. Chen put the Lang to his shoulder, cocked the other hammer, and asked, 'What is it, Mrs Baxter?'

Sarah, who had been just inside the door, came out on to the porch and picked up the papers. After she'd read them, she crushed them into a ball and threw it at Hollister. 'You can go to hell, you fat tub of lard, you—'

'Sarah,' said Helen, 'your language.'

'—but, Mama, he claims Pap sold the ranch. It's a lie.'

Helen was past her initial shock. She stepped off of the porch and retrieved the notice and un-crumpled it. 'This is signed by Judge Miller. I know he's friendly with Griffin, but he wouldn't put his name on this,' she held up the notice, 'unless he believed it was true that Luke sold the ranch.'

'Yes, ma'am.'

'What proof does he have?' asked Helen.

Hollister paused and then said, 'Griffin has a bill-of-sale with your husband's signature on it.'

'—and the judge believes Luke actually signed it?'

Helen's eyes and lips were slits as she stared at the sheriff. She asked, 'Who witnessed the signature?'

Hollister flinched, it was involuntary, and he hoped she hadn't seen it. 'I'm not at liberty to talk about the details. You'll have to take it up with the judge.'

Helen responded through clenched teeth. 'I'll take it up with the governor.'

Not sure how to answer, Hollister said, 'ma'am.' With that, he tapped the brim of his hat, reined his horse from the house, and started the long ride back to Charlo.

'Mama, we can't just let them take our home.'

Helen put her arm around her daughter's shoulder.

'Sweetheart, this has to be a mistake. I don't know how, but Griffin has got Judge Miller on his side. We've thirty days, so if I'm to speak with the governor we need to get started.'

She scanned the barn and corral. The ring of hammer to steel drew her attention to the blacksmith's lean-to. It was Gus shaping shoes for a horse.

'Gus,' she called. On her third call, Gus looked toward the house and saw Helen on the porch. She waved for him to come.

She watched the hard-muscled man make his way to the house. He looked up to the porch, scratched his bearded cheek, and asked, 'You wanted to see me, Mrs Baxter?'

'Yes, Gus, I did. Please make arrangements for you and one of the men to accompany me to Butte. We'll leave in the morning.'

'Yes, ma'am,' he said and turned back toward the barn.

'Gus,' Helen called. He stopped and looked back. 'I'll be going dressed as a lady, so please prepare the buckboard.'

With a sheepish grin, he said, 'Yes, ma'am.'

'Mama, do you think it wise to travel in the open like that?'

Helen could read the concern on her daughter's face. 'Sarah, Griffin doesn't think he needs to take that kind of chance. He plans to let a corrupt government do his dirty work. But you just wait and see.'

Three days later, Helen Baxter was again sitting in the governor's anteroom. This time, she had to wait like the others before he saw her. In the afternoon of her second day, the clerk led her into the governor's office.

He rose and came around his desk to greet her. 'How nice it is to see you again, Helen. Please, won't you have a seat?'

Helen smiled cordially, and took the offered seat. 'Thank you, Benjamin.'

He sat across from her. 'What can I do for you, Helen?'

She handed him the eviction notice. He glanced at it. 'I wired Griffin and Judge Miller when you arrived. The judge has seen the bill-of-sale and believes it to be genuine.'

'I thought as much,' she said. 'But it's a forgery. It has to be. Luke would never have contemplated selling the Box-B without discussing it with me.'

'Sometimes men do make decisions without their wives, Helen.'

She bristled at his condescension, her jaw clenched, but she forced herself to be calm as she spoke. 'I am aware of that, Benjamin, but he didn't even mention that an offer had been made. Luke would never have sold the ranch without at least telling me.'

'Maybe he wanted to surprise you?'

Her eyes sparked, and her voice developed an edge.

'Benjamin, I am aware that it has been many years since we kept company, but I haven't changed that much – if at all. Do you really think I'd marry a man who made those kinds of decisions without my knowledge?'

Potts stood and began to pace his office. At length, he left off and returned to his chair. 'No, Helen. I do not believe you'd marry a man who would do that to you under any circumstance. However, Judge Miller has a witnessed bill-of-sale that he believes to be genuine. He may not be the best man for the job, but I believe he is honest and respects the law.'

'Did he say who witnessed the document?' she asked.

He rose and went to his desk to review the telegrams. 'He did not, but I can find out. Give me a few hours. Where are you staying?'

'My men and I are staying at the Valley Lake Hotel.'

'Stay there and I'll send word when I hear something. Now please, if you'll excuse me.'

Helen left Potts' office feeling encouraged.

'Griffin, I've received another telegram from the governor. He wants to know who witnessed the document.'

'How could that make a difference?' asked Griffin.

'I don't know that it does,' said Miller, 'but he's the governor, and he wants to know.'

Griffin's jaw began to tighten. 'When will I be done with this woman and her persistent avoidance?'

'I'm sure the governor is just confirming the details.'

'I paid Baxter $108,000 cash. Murphy told me that Mrs Baxter settled her bill at the general store, and the banker said she's no longer in arears with their cattle loan. Where'd the money come from if I didn't buy the ranch? Tell that to the governor.'

Miller gave Griffin time to calm down before he said, 'I'll give him that information along with Sheriff Hollister's name. Thank you, Web, I'll see myself out.'

Outside Griffin's office, the sun was at its hottest time of the day. Miller walked to the telegraph office to reply to the governor's request for information. Along the way, his mind reviewed the situation; he felt like he was in court and deciding on a verdict.

Griffin was agitated about the governor having Hollister's name. *Could it be because Hollister does what Griffin tells him to do? There have been rumors about Griffin's other deals in the county. What about the Baxter family? I didn't know Luke Baxter that well, but he seemed like a decent fella, and highly thought of by the community. But, then. . . .*

'Thank you for coming here to the hotel,' said Helen. 'I know you're busy. I would have been happy to return to your office.'

Potts wouldn't meet her stare; he fidgeted with the telegram held in his hands. He pulled it through his fingers one edge at a time working his way around the square. Eventually, he said, 'Helen, I've heard back from Judge Miller.'

She watched Potts closely; she chewed her lower lip all the while twisting her wedding ring round her finger. Oh, how I wish Luke were here. . . . 'Benjamin, out with it, please.'

At last, he looked her in the eyes. 'The information is a bit conflicting.'

'And—'

'Sheriff Hollister witnessed the signature. Though he has

no proof to the contrary, he feels that's not as solid as it might otherwise seem.'

She sighed with relief, stopped worrying her ring, and beamed him with a huge grin. 'Ha! I knew it. I just knew it. Hollister is on Griffin's payroll and does what he's told.'

'Helen, there is another issue that's worrisome.'

She sobered. 'Go on,' she said and inhaled deeply holding her breath.

'It's seems that you've come into a good deal of money as of late. Paid your creditors and your note at the bank is now current. If your husband didn't sell the ranch where did the money come from?'

Helen exhaled and a smile returned to her face. 'Oh that's easy to explain. I have an investor. Chen Lee, our cook, is part owner of the ranch.'

Potts pinched his brow and bent his head slightly to the right, and asked, 'Your cook?'

'Certainly,' she said. 'He was with my husband before we married and our family since. He's saved his money and with all the problems and the cattle rustling. . . .'

'Helen, don't you realize how unbelievable that sounds? You've made your Chinese cook a business partner.'

Blood rose up her neck and pinked her cheeks, her eyes flashed. 'How dare you suggest—'

Potts raised his hands. 'Helen, please. I'm just saying that it's hard to believe, that's all.'

'Well, you can ask anyone in Charlo that knows Chen, and they'll confirm the kind of man he is, and, and—' She clamped her mouth shut; it formed a thin line across her face.

He issued a long low sigh and bowed his head. 'All right, Helen, I've known you all these years. I'll look into this further, but I can't make any promises.'

Helen reached out and patted his knee. 'Thank you, Benjamin, that's all I wanted, a fair chance.'

The governor stood. 'If you'll excuse me, I still have work that needs my attention yet this afternoon.' She watched him leave. *He doesn't seem happy for me, or is it that he has to confront Griffin and his money?*

Helen's high spirits were contagious. Karl sat his saddle a little taller. Gus, who drove the buckboard, seemed animated and wore a smile. *He's not unattractive when he smiles,* she thought.

The telegraph operator jingled his five silver dollars. 'Thank you, sir. Jus' thought you'd want to know what the judge sent to the governor.'

Griffin nodded and waved him away. As he began to read the telegram, his expression scowled.

ON THE SURFACE EVERYTHING APPEARS LEGAL STOP SHERIFF HOLLISTER WITNESSED THE SIGNATURE STOP HOLLISTER IS GRIFFIN'S MAN STOP HAVE CONCERNS ABOUT HOLLISTER STOP ALSO CONCERNED WITH MRS BAXTER STOP SHE HAS PAID OFF CREDITORS AND NOTE AT BANK NOW CURRENT STOP NO KNOWN SOURCE FOR MONEY EXCEPT HUSBAND'S POSSIBLE SALE OF RANCH STOP

Griffin relaxed and smiled when he read the last sentence.

He had no idea where she got the money, but it worked in his favor. If only he didn't have to depend on Hollister.

CHAPTER 10

With the afternoon sun behind his back, the lone rider crested the ridge. He slouched in his saddle as if asleep.

'Whoa,' called Big Mose. 'That you, Toots?'

Toots reined in as the big man approached. 'Howdy, Mose.'

Mose offered his hand to Toots. 'Thought it was you. Couldn't make you out, but I knowed your horse.' Without giving Toots a chance to return the greeting, Mose plowed ahead. 'Did you get that sum-bitch Danton?'

Toots replied. 'Yep, him and the two that rode with 'im.' Toots stood in his stirrups and rubbed his lower back. 'I sure am lookin' forward to sleepin' indoors and eatin' decent food.'

Big Mose grinned. 'Miss Sarah's goin' to be mighty pleased to see ya back. She spends most all her time every-day watchin' the ridgeline hopin' to see ya.'

Toots smiled; he still had a little ways to go before he could make out people's faces, but he searched for Sarah's. 'Later Mose,' he said and nudged Knothead toward home.

Twenty minutes later, he spied Sarah; at least, he thought it was her. From his distance from the main house, she looked no taller than a prairie dog on watch for birds of

94

prey. As he rode closer, she waved. Boot heels to his pony's flanks brought Toots at a gallop to the front porch and Sarah.

As Knothead slid to a halt, Toots came out of his saddle. Sarah bound down the porch steps, threw her arms around his neck, and gave him a wet kiss on the mouth.

She said, 'I've been so worried. Gone more 'an two weeks and no word.' She stepped back and looked him up and down. 'Are you all right? You look fine. Need to shave and take a bath, but otherwise—'

'Sarah,' said Helen. 'Let him say a word or two.'

Sarah's eyes welled, her lower lip trembled, and then she threw herself at him and squeezed him tight.

Toots stumbled from the force of her emotion-driven onslaught, but caught himself before they fell to the ground. With wide eyes and opened mouth, he looked to the smiling faces of Helen and Chen still on the porch. After a few seconds, he put his arms around Sarah and squeezed.

'I missed you too, Sarah. I didn't realize how much 'til now.'

'Sarah, release him. I'm sure he's tired and hungry.' She looked at Toots. 'Suppers on; come into the kitchen for coffee.'

She was reluctant to release him, but Sarah let go. Her compromise was to take his arm and lead him into the kitchen, where she busied herself serving him coffee. Helen sat a bottle of Canadian whiskey on the table.

'When my husband came home from a long trip, he liked to have some with his coffee. He said it helped relax his muscles.'

Toots gave her a grateful smile and poured himself a generous splash into his cup. 'That it does, ma'am.'

Helen let out a heavy sigh. 'Would you please call me Helen?'

Toots glanced at Chen and then Sarah. 'Well, ma'am, I'll try, but ma'am is more comfortable for me – don't mean no disrespect.'

'As you wish,' she said. 'You and Chen certainly are stubborn about how I'm to be addressed.'

A quick glance from Toots saw Chen grinning; it was the first time he'd seen the Chinaman act so familiar.

'Did you kill Danton?' asked Sarah.

'Sarah!' said Helen with a stern harshness in her tone.

Toots flinched, but Sarah ignored her mother's rebuke.

'Well, did you kill him?' Sarah asked again.

He poured more whiskey into his now empty cup and knocked it back. Followed by a deep breath, he felt the tingling burn inch down his windpipe and began to warm his stomach.

His expression grew somber as he provided the details of his trip. When he told of Danton's confession, Sarah interrupted.

'I knew I was right about that skunk,' said Sarah, her jaw set firm. 'I'm glad he's dead. Now we got to get Griffin.'

Helen reached out, and put a hand on her daughter's shoulder. 'Sarah, please don't hate like that – it's not healthy.'

'I'll stop when Griffin is dead; until then. . . .'

Toots continued. Helen smiled when she heard what Mr Roberts said. 'We don't know him well,' she said, 'but he's always treated us fair when we've conducted business.'

Finished, he asked, 'Anythin' happen here while I was gone?'

Helen and Sarah looked at one another, Chen turned away to the stove and supper's preparation.

'Well?' he asked.

Sarah opened her mouth to speak, but her mother placed

a hand on her arm, which silenced her.

'We've been served with an eviction notice,' said Helen.

Everyone looked at Toots. Sarah held his hand; Helen bit her lower lip, and Chen turned from the stove.

'How can that be? Don't you own the ranch?'

'We do,' said Helen with a glance to Chen. 'However, Griffin claims he has a signed bill-of-sale from Luke, witnessed by Sheriff Hollister.'

'Is it bona fide?' asked Toots.

'I don't believe it is. Luke would never have sold this place and certainly not without talking to me first.'

'Griffin's lyin' and Hollister's swearin' to it.' Toots was on his feet now, pacing the kitchen. 'I figured Hollister for lookin' the other way, but I didn't think he'd go this far.'

Helen offered, 'I've spoken to Governor Potts, but he's reluctant to accept my word that the bill-of-sale is a forgery. However, he did agree to look further into our situation. We've got three weeks left.'

Chen began to set food on the table. 'I suggest we eat supper and let Toots get some rest. We can talk again in the morning.'

When the oven door opened the aroma of turkey filled the kitchen. 'Mmm, the smell,' said Toots, 'I can't remember the last time I had turkey.'

'Your return is timed well,' said Helen. 'Gus bagged two birds this morning. Chen's cooked them both; he's already taken one to the bunkhouse as you were arriving.'

Toots winked at Chen. 'Now, I know why the hands didn't come out to say hello.'

Chen placed the carving knife on the table. 'Toots, would you like to carve the bird?'

Toots's brow wrinkled; he pulled his ear, and looked away. 'Chen, I'm afraid I don't know the proper way to cut it up.

If we was on the trail, I'd just pull off a chunk and start eatin'.'

'If you like, Toots,' said Helen, 'I'd be happy to show you the way Luke use to do it. Then you can do it next time.'

'Next time?' asked Toots.

Sarah said, 'Pap would take the Lang and go hunting at least once a week. Grouse, pheasant, or turkey when they're around – he just about always brought somethin' home. A person can only eat so much beef.'

Helen filled his plate. 'I made rhubarb pie for dessert, so save room.'

He grinned. 'Ma'am, I've always got room for pies and such.'

After pie and coffee, Toots and Sarah sat on the porch for a spell watching the sunset. She held his hand and sat close. 'Toots—' she paused. 'I don't want to upset you, but would it be all right if I called you William or Bill?'

'Some people call me McGee. Would that be easier for you?'

'I'd rather use William, but if you insist.' Then her eyes squinted, and her mouth became a straight line curled down at the corners. She took a deep breath and blurted, 'If we're goin' to marry then I'm goin' to call you William.'

Toots's mouth fell open, and he stared at her. His eyes blinked rapidly. His mouth began to move, but he uttered no words. At length, he found his voice. 'Sarah, I—' He fell silent.

Sarah turned and searched his eyes; her shoulders curved forward as she clutched at her breast. 'You do want to marry me, don't you?' She held her breath as she chewed her lower lip.

In the fleeting sun light, he could just make out the flecks of gold sparkling in the chestnut color of her eyes. They drew him forward, and he kissed her wet lips.

'Ouch,' she said and jerked back touching her lips. 'You poked me with your beard.'

Dismayed by the interruption, he put his hands to his moustache and beard, and tried to smooth the stubble down, without success. 'Do you want me to go shave?'

Sarah leaned forward and pecked his lips. 'It's like kissin' a prickly pear. You got to dodge the prickly to get the pears. If you're goin' to kiss me every day you have to shave every day.'

The sun was down, and the only light came from the glow of the parlor lamp inside the house. The light flickered in her expectant stare as she smiled at him. Toots wasn't quite sure how it had happened, but now, he was engaged. As he gave it further thought, he decided he liked the idea.

'How'd you know I'd get hitched; I didn't know my own self?'

Sarah tilted her head back and fingered her hair back over her shoulder to expose her face. Her smile was coy, she said, 'Women know these things.' That was all she said on the matter.

'Well, I guess I'd better speak to your ma.' He glanced through the window to see if Helen was there; she sat darning clothes. 'And of course, there's this business with Griffin to be settled afore we can do anything proper.'

'Mama's been waitin' for you to talk to her for a while now.'

'Huh?'

'Oh, she's known all along that you wanted to marry me.'

'Just when was that?'

Sarah's eyes twinkled with delightful mischief. 'Mama said she suspected it when you agreed to be our foreman. She could tell that you wanted to say no, but you changed your mind. It was your feelin's for me. I mean that's what made you say yes.'

Toots thought back; at the time, it seemed the right thing to do, but he said, 'I recall wanting to help you and your mother – even after you shot me.'

She recoiled, but when she saw his playful expression she punched him in the stomach. He grabbed after her, but she was too quick and twisted away to her feet. She looked through the door. 'Mama's in the parlor—'

Toots was up earlier than the others. Even though it wasn't Saturday, he decided to have a bath. There was a washroom attached to the bunkhouse. It had a board counter with six ceramic washbowls along one wall, and a single galvanized tub for a total bath. In the far corner, stood a potbellied cast-iron stove to remove the winter chill and heat water.

After his bath, while his whiskers were soft, he shaved. Bare to the waist, he inspected himself. His face and neck were a reddish brown; his forearms and hands were the same. He touched the purple scar on his freckled white shoulder. *Mrs Baxter did a good job of sewin'. It won't be no time at all and it'll be hard to see.*

At breakfast, when Toots came through the kitchen door, Helen and Sarah stared at him with smiles. He wore her brother's clothes, which Helen insisted he take.

Sarah came from the table and kissed his cheek. 'That's much better.' On impulse, she ran her fingers through his hair. 'Who trimmed you hair?'

'Little Mose. He costs less than the barber and he's closer.'

'Breakfast is ready,' said Helen. 'Come and sit down.'

After breakfast, they cleared the table and discussed the eviction notice. 'We know the bill-of-sale is a forgery,' said

Toots. 'We just need to figure how to prove it.'

Helen stared off into the distance, lost in thought. 'The sheriff didn't bring the bill-of-sale with him, so I can't know if it's Luke's signature or not.'

'Hollister is the key to this situation,' said Chen. It was his first contribution to their meeting. 'If we are to suppose that the witnessed sale is a forgery, then Hollister lied about being a witness. He doesn't strike me as a man of real mettle.'

'If he had sand, he wouldn't be Griffin's lackey,' said Toots, contempt thick in his voice. 'I'm thinkin' I'll take a ride into Charlo, see what Hollister has to say.'

Sarah reached out and placed her hand on Toots's arm. 'You're not goin' alone are you?'

He patted her hand. 'No, I figured on takin' Gus with me.'

Outside of town, Toots reined in. 'I think I'll circle around town, and make my way to Hollister's office without bein' noticed. Give me twenty minutes and then you ride into town and hole up at Murphy's store. If there's trouble, you'll be close enough to know. When I leave, I'll ride by the store.'

Gus pulled out his watch and clicked open the case. 'Good luck, Toots. If there's any shootin' I'll come a-runnin', and if you don't show in an hour or so, I'll come to see why.'

'Thanks,' said Toots as he reined east to skirt the town.

The jailhouse was at the center of town, caddy-corner across the street from Murphy's store. Toots rode in from the east. Grass-roofed sod houses were the first structures he came upon. A few had tin roofs, but it was a shabby place to live. It was the town's underbelly, the people who lived there clung to their meager existence. They stared at him with dark sinister eyes.

Two streets closer to the jailhouse, the houses were wood framed with clapboard siding and glass in their windows. The townsfolk who lived here were the employees of the town. Their children played in their yards, small plots of grassless dirt.

There was a corral that served the saloon two doors up from the jailhouse. He left his horse there. He moved down the alley on the north side of the only solid brick building in town, and watched the street. When the traffic broke, Toots hopped on to the boardwalk and walked the few steps to Hollister's office. It was morning, so he'd still be there.

Toots peered through the small window in the top of the heavy wood door. A fat man stood by the stove pouring coffee. He fit the description given, so Toots opened the door and walked in.

The sheriff's head snapped toward Toots, but he held on to the coffee pot. 'What's your business, sonny.'

Toots smiled, wanting the sheriff to be at ease. 'You Sheriff Hollister?'

CHAPTER 11

The sheriff nodded. 'State your business, son.'

'My name's Toots McGee, foreman over to the Box-B.'

Hollister's jaw tensed and his eyes hooded. He set the pot back on to the stove. Eyes fixed on Toots, he returned to his desk and sat down his cup. 'You the fellow Danton tangled with?'

'It's handy you brung him up, I come to parley about him.'

'That so?'

'Danton and me had a long talk afore he died. Why don't you take a seat an' I'll tell you what all he had to say?'

Hollister eased his gun hand toward his hip.

'Sheriff, that's the same mistake Danton made. Why don't you take that seat, keep your hands where I can see 'em, and we'll talk.'

Toots saw beads of sweat on the sheriff's forehead. His shoulders remained hunched as he considered takin' action, but in the end, he relaxed; hands on the desktop, he sat.

'Did you get Crazy Bill and Hank Springer too?'

'They didn't give me no choice. It was them or me.'

The sheriff's mouth dropped out and his eyes widened. 'You mean to tell me that you kilt all three by yourself?'

'Like I said, they didn't give me no choice.'

The sheriff's hand moved to the center of his desk, and

he laced his fingers together. 'What'd Danton have to say?'

'Plenty, Sheriff. He says you're on Griffin's payroll and looked the other way when he killed Luke Baxter and his son. There have been others too.'

'Those killin's happened outside my jurisdiction.' Hollister's brow glistened, and he squeezed his laced fingers until the knuckles turned white. 'There was nothin' I could do about 'em.'

'—but it's in your jurisdiction to serve eviction papers based on a forged bill-of-sale that you witnessed.'

'Now look here. Judge Miller had me to deliver 'em papers.' He paused. 'What makes you think the bill-of-sale is fake?'

Toots gave him a pleasant smile. ''Cause Danton was at the last meeting Baxter had with Griffin. Baxter told Griffin to go to hell. He'd never sell the Box-B. Danton followed 'em and when they were near home, he bushwhacked 'em. There's no way the sale is bona fide.'

The sheriff's hands trembled, and he sleeved the sweat from his brow. 'You can't prove none of that.'

'Well, maybe I can't, or just maybe I got a signed deathbed confession in my pocket.' Toots patted his chest for theatrics.

'What do you expect me to do?' asked the sheriff.

Toots had him. 'I think you should write out a confession to your part in Griffin's crimes. Then, pack up your possibles and quit Charlo. I suggest you move back east where it's tamer.'

'What if I say no?'

Eyes hooded, Toots stared at the sheriff; an aura of death emitted from his being. 'Then shuck your iron and we'll dance.'

'You're bluffin',' said Hollister, his voice lacking confidence.

Toots put his hand on the butt of his Colt. 'No one knows I'm in town, nor saw me come into your office.'

Hollister raised his hands palms out. 'You win, I'll do it.'

He opened the center drawer, but before his hand moved to the drawer, Toots pulled and cocked the Colt. 'Paper better be the only thin' in your hands when I see 'em.'

With great care, Hollister withdrew a sheet of paper. Pen and ink were already on the desk. He wrote for several minutes then signed the document. Finished, he handed it to Toots to read.

'You're lowdown, Sheriff. Was you ever honest?'

Hollister bowed his head. 'There was a time—'

Toots folded the paper and put it in his pocket, stepped backwards to the door and looked out the window. The street was clear, but for Gus standin' in front of Murphy's. 'Sheriff, I got people on the street. I suggest you sip that coffee for a spell afore you leave your office.' Hollister nodded.

Toots moved fast and was out the door and to his pony in less than a minute. He reined on to Main Street and galloped north out of town. At the first stand of cottonwoods, he halted and rode between them for concealment while he watched the road.

Gus reined in when Toots rode out from the trees. Gus grinned. 'Son, you must've put the fear of God into Hollister.'

'Why?'

'I waited near fifteen minutes afore he stuck his head through the door and looked around. He didn't see me 'cause I was inside Murphy's. Anyhows, he lit out for Griffin's office like his pants was afire. It was damned funny.'

Toots smiled at the image Gus's words conjured. 'Let's get back to the ranch afore we have unwanted company.'

Knothead whinnied at the repeated use of spurs, but galloped off without further protest.

*

105

Helen read Hollister's confession for the third time; the first two times aloud for all to hear. She folded the paper with care and placed it in her apron pocket, and patted it as she spoke, 'It's done. When we show this to the judge, he'll have to rescind the conviction notice and take action against Griffin.'

'I ain't so sure it'll be that easy, Mrs Baxter,' said Toots. 'Hollister's got no choice but to quit Charlo, and make his-self hard to find. Without 'im, I don't expect the judge'll do the right thing.'

Helen sighed. 'I think Sarah has a point.'

Toots wrinkled his brow and cocked his head pointing an ear towards her. 'Beg your pardon, ma'am.'

'Well, since you're going to become a member of the family, I agree with Sarah that we should call you William. And, if you'll allow me, I'd like to work with you on your grammar.'

Chen stepped outside leaving Sarah, Helen, and Toots to discuss the situation. 'Well, ma'am. . . .'

Helen sat down at the table and placed her hands toward Toots. 'Let's begin there. I would prefer that you address me as Helen and, after you two are married: mother.'

Toots glanced at Sarah. Her smile told him she wouldn't be coming to his aid. 'Ma – Helen – I guess I ain't got no objections to betterin' myself, but—'

Helen's smile was disarming as she interrupted. '—you haven't any objection to improving yourself.'

'That's what I said.'

Sarah giggled.

Helen's stare of rebuke stopped her giggle. 'I'll have none of that, Sarah.'

'Yes, Mother.'

'Now then, William,' said Helen with a triumphant smile. 'I do think we should make a trip to town to see Judge Miller.'

Chen, who had been listening at the door returned to the kitchen 'May I suggest we wait a week or so to see what happens? When Hollister tells Griffin about Danton, and Danton's confession, he may well abandon his plans and leave town.'

Toots stroked his face with his left hand several times. He tried without success to reduce his growing frustration. 'Chen, you're ill-informed about Griffin. He'll not stop 'til he's won or dead – not before.'

'We'll deal with your language later, William. Meanwhile, what do you suggest?' asked Helen.

He grimaced at the formality of the name, but responded anyway. 'We wait as Chen says, but we also get word to the governor that we can prove Griffin killed your husband and son.'

Helen's eyes welled at the mention of her husband and son's murder. Sarah moved to stand by her mother, she hugged her and stroked her back to sooth her sorrow.

Toots felt awkward at the display of emotion. 'I'm terrible sorry, ma'am – I mean Helen. It weren't my intentions to make you feel sorrowful an' all—'

She showed him a brave smile. 'William, my dear, you need never to apologize to me for talking about my husband and son. You've single-handedly done more to give us justice for their murders than anyone, and I'll be forever grateful.'

He stood; he had no idea how to respond, or how to act. Head bowed, his voice gentle, he said, 'Helen, I need to think on this for a spell. 'He walked out through the kitchen door bent on going to the corral to find his horse. Knothead proved to be a good listener, and helped him resolve many problems.

Toots had been on his own for a long time, his father never came home from the war and his mother died of a fever. At first, he moved from one neighbor to the next. At each, he worked for his room and board. In his middle teens, he started drifting and learned to be a cowboy.

He could read and write, thanks to his mother, and he had a good sense for numbers, but he'd never thought to be a rancher. That would change if he survived the fight with Griffin.

Knothead dropped his head over the rail and prodded Toots for attention. 'Yeah, I know – you miss the trail. It appears we've found a home, Knot; a bride and family to go with it too.'

He stroked his horse's neck as he spoke. As if in reply, Knothead whinnied and nodded toward the house. Toots smiled. 'Well, if you agree, it's settled.'

With things worked out in his mind, he strolled into the bunkhouse, and the most peaceful night's sleep he could recall.

'Good morning, William,' said Helen. 'You seem well rested and rather chipper.'

His smile grew to a huge grin. 'Yes, ma'am, I slept tighter 'an tick on a dog's back.'

Helen chuckled. 'I'm not quite sure what that phrase means, but I assume you're telling me that you slept well.'

He nodded and turned to Sarah. 'I was thinkin' we could go for a ride after breakfast?'

'Oh yes, that would be wonderful,' said Sarah.

Helen and Chen gave smiles of encouragement and exchanged knowing glances. 'William,' began Helen, 'I have given a great deal of thought to what you had to say, and I agree. We shall wait for Griffin's next move and respond accordingly. Meanwhile, we'll get a message to Governor Potts, but how?'

Toots rubbed the back of his neck. His mouth grimaced as he searched for a solution. He shrugged. 'The only thing I can think of is to ride to the next stage way station after Charlo and post a letter from there. Little Mose could get there and back in a day, easy.'

Helen considered. 'All right, I'll write the letter, and I will start it tonight. I'll give it to you when it's finished.'

The wind blew through Sarah's hair as they raced across the valley toward the lake. At the water's edge, they slowed their horses to a walk and traveled along the lake's bank northwest upward into the pines and seclusion, their conversation mute as they rode, each comfortable with the other.

'When do you think this will finally be finished, William?'

It dawned on him that when Sarah called him William, it seemed correct. 'I ain't got a notion of when exactly; I reckon it'll be when Griffin calls it quits, or is dead.'

Sarah reined to a halt and stared at him; grave concern filled her eyes. 'Do you have to be the one who kills Griffin?'

The muscles of his face slackened with resigned acceptance of the future task. 'I expect so.'

'Oh,' said Sarah with gentle resolve. She nudged her mount forward and looked to the sky. 'It's so peaceful and beautiful up here by the lake. I know we need to be at the ranch for work and all, but could we have a small cabin up here – just for us after we're married?'

For the first time since she'd told him they would marry, he didn't panic. In fact, he felt ardent, willing, even excited about their marriage prospects. 'All these tall pines – it won't be fancy, but it'll be warm and comfortable. I'll get started just as soon as things is settled.'

CHAPTER 12

Hollister's big belly quivered as he hurried to Griffin's office. He'd hung back not so much in fear of Toots as he needed to decide what he'd tell Griffin.

Without permission to enter, he stormed into Griffin's office. A wide-eyed glance of the room assured him that Griffin was alone. 'Mr Griffin, that McGee fella just left the jail.'

Griffin had looked up when Hollister burst into his office. 'What are you goin' on about, Sheriff?'

'McGee, the fella who tangled with Tom, works for the Box-B.'

It took a moment for him to translate what Hollister was saying. 'What's that to do with me?'

Hollister looked at Griffin as if he didn't understand plain English. 'He's kilt Danton and the two men with him – claims Danton signed a confession about the thing's he done for you.'

Now he had Griffin's attention. He jumped to his feet. 'Sheriff, you're tellin' me that you let him leave town?'

Hollister decided to lie. He'd decided to lie about most of what had happened, and then when it suited his needs sneak out of town. 'He'd pulled his Colt on me, Mr Griffin. The hole in the end of that lead pusher looks mighty big at close range.'

'What'd he say?'

The sheriff parsed in his mind the information he planned to share. 'McGee said I was to stay away with the eviction notice on account he had Danton's confession – claims Danton told him, he kilt Baxter, and the boy, afore any sale could've took place.'

Griffin walked to his liquor cabinet and poured himself a generous glass of whiskey. When he turned, he saw Hollister staring at his glass. 'Help yourself, Sheriff.'

Hollister stepped to the cabinet, and matched Griffin's pour and took a long drink. He inhaled deep at the burn in his throat, but soon enough, he felt it warm his belly and fortify his flagging courage.

'What're we goin' to do?' asked Hollister. Griffin sipped his whiskey lost in thought. 'Mr Griffin—'

Griffin looked at the sheriff. 'I think he's bluffin', Sheriff. Oh, Danton may have told him things, but he doesn't have a written confession. If he had, he'd have gone to Judge Miller, not you.'

Hollister paled. Oh shit, he thought.

'What is it, Sheriff? You look like you seen a ghost?'

'—but what if he ain't bluffin'? Then what?'

'King Malone.'

'That gunman who kilt 'em men in the Colorado range war?'

'Yeah. I sent for him the day after Danton pulled out. I expect Malone to be here any day.'

The sheriff paled again. This is gettin' worse. I'd better make my plans to get out now. Hollister decided it was time to leave Griffin's office, so he made for the door.

Griffin said, 'Where you goin', Sheriff?'

Hollister halted, but didn't turn to face Griffin. 'I got paper work at the office needs tendin'. Griffin, I'm thinkin' about goin' fishin' afore this Malone fella gets here.'

'That might be a good idea, Sheriff. If you're out of town things would move along with greater ease. I'd say about two weeks should do.'

The next afternoon, Griffin sat at his desk. He read newspapers from back east. The information was two weeks old, but he was still better informed than most of the other businessmen of the territory.

Page came into his office, pale-faced and his expression drawn. There were beads of sweat on his brow; he'd hurried. Something or someone spooked him. 'There's a man in the Spoke – says he's King Malone.' Page swallowed hard. 'He says you're to come there now.'

Griffin carefully folded his newspaper and placed it on his desk. He let out a slow breath and sighed. 'Please tell Mr Malone I'll be along directly.'

'—but, he said—'

'You've delivered the message, Page. I suggest you get back to work.'

Page turned to the door then stopped. 'I don't mean no disrespect, but do you know who King Malone is?'

Griffin looked up, his eyes flinty. 'I sent for him. Now do as I say.'

Page pulled the bar towel from his shoulder and wiped the perspiration from the top of his shiny head and then scurried away through the door.

I guess I'll have to set the rules for Mr Malone.

At the Broken Spoke, he peered over the batwing doors and scanned the room. Toward the rear, seated at a table under the balcony and stationed to see all the room's entries, sat King Malone.

As Griffin walked toward the table, he sized up the man. Not yet thirty, Malone was clean-shaven, dressed in a dark suit, his hat creased into a low crown. When Griffin reached the table, he could see the matched pair of ivory-handled Colts: one in its holster tied to his right leg, and the other in a cross draw rig, its leather keeper loop off the hammer.

Griffin eased his jacket open and hooked his thumbs in the pockets of his vest. He asked, 'Mr Malone?' The man nodded and then glanced at a chair. 'Mr Malone, I conduct business at my office. If you wish to see me, you may do so there.' Griffin turned, walked along the bar, nodded at Page, and out the doors.

On return to his office, he told his clerk that a Mr Malone would arrive soon, and that he was to be shown in without delay. Five minutes later Malone was in his office doorway.

'Mr Malone, thank you for responding to my wire so quickly. Would you like coffee or something stronger? I have Canadian whiskey.'

Malone surveyed the room; he then dragged a straight-backed chair to where he could watch Griffin, including the window behind him, and the office door. 'Black coffee will do.'

Griffin poured him a cup and set it on the corner of his desk within Malone's reach.

'Your wire said $500 when I arrived. I'm here.'

'Aw, so it did,' said Griffin, and he reached for his desk draw. Malone's hand moved to his belly gun, and Griffin froze. 'I understand your caution, but really . . . do you seriously think I have a weapon in this drawer?'

The gunman stood and moved around the desk. With his left on the draw pull, he paused when Griffin spoke.

'Let me rephrase that. Do you really think I would pull

that gun on you? I assure you I have no need or desire to own your reputation.'

Malone opened the drawer to expose a cash box and a large caliber Derringer. His eyes looked up at Griffin, and he smiled. 'You'd have to be standin' next to me to kill me with that.'

Griffin returned the smile. 'It's more for peace of mind than anything else. That's why I've hired your services.'

Malone removed the cash box, placed it on the desk, and closed the drawer. Griffin opened it and hefted a small bag; its contents clinked when he dropped it on the desk. He released the tie and spilled out twenty-five gold double eagles. 'Five hundred dollars as agreed.'

Malone scooped up the coins and dropped them back into the bag; he counted each as they clinked. 'Who gets kilt?'

Griffin's smile showing his satisfaction with the prospect, he said, 'A young man, who goes by the name of Toots McGee.'

Malone's eyes widened slightly as he looked at Griffin. 'Red hair?' he asked.

'Yes. Why do you ask?'

The gunman smiled, but it carried no friendliness. 'There was some shootin' over cattle in Colorado a year or so back. A red-headed fella named McGee came out on top.'

'I didn't think he was a professional gunman,' said Griffin.

'He's not,' said Malone. 'He's just good with his gun. I'm better.'

'I don't want him bushwhacked. I can get that done for far less than five hundred dollars. It has to look like a fair fight to the town.'

Malone smiled, but it still held no friendliness; it

114

reminded Griffin of a coiled snake lying in wait. 'I know how to do my job.'

Toots lingered over his coffee at the kitchen table. Chen stepped out of the pantry. 'We need supplies.'

'Make a list, Chen, an' I'll go into town for you.'

Chen lifted his leg and moved it in several directions. 'My leg is fine. I can go to town.'

'—but it could be dangerous.'

'I don't see how. You've taken care of Danton and his men. Griffin doesn't want a repeat of that sort of problem. I'll be fine.'

'Well maybe I'll ride along. Being foreman keeps a man too busy to go to town on Saturdays. Besides, I might want to buy somethin' special from the dry goods store.'

Chen looked at him knowingly, he asked. 'A gift for Sarah?'

Color came to his face and he flinched at Chen's words. Toots hadn't as yet gotten comfortable with others speaking about their engagement. 'Well, we're engaged you know. I thought I'd look at ribbons and such – maybe Mrs Murphy could help me.'

Chen's expression sobered and he looked back toward the storeroom. 'I'll be ready to go by the time the wagon's hitched.'

The wagon bumped along with Chen at the reins, and Toots straddled Knothead. It was a pleasant ride. Toots rode alongside the wagon and daydreamed about a life with Sarah on the Box-B.

'You've never been married, Chen?' asked Toots.

Chen exhaled with a sigh, and his eyes stared at the distance. 'Sadly no, I have not been married. My bride to be and I were separated when I was shanghaied.'

115

'Shanghaied?' asked Toots.

Toots spent the remainder of the ride hanging on to every word Chen spoke as he told about his meeting and subsequent adventures with Luke Baxter.

It was after lunchtime when they arrived. Like most cowboys, especially the younger ones, he was hungry. 'What do you say to my standin' you the cost of a meal at the café?'

'I've lived here nearly thirty years,' said Chen, 'I've never been inside the café, the hotel, or the saloons.'

'I'd say it's high time we change that,' said Toots, and they strolled off toward the Blue Bell Café. As they stepped through the door, the patrons looked on and hushed their conversations.

A grin to match Toots's jaunty mood spread across his face, and he led them to a table near the kitchen's doorway. The waitress, a thick blonde girl whose face normally held a smile, frowned as she approached. Her eyes darted around the room and in a low voice, she said, 'Please, we don't want any trouble.'

'Why would you expect trouble?' asked Toots. His brow began to pinch with his left eyebrow lower than the right as he eyed the girl. 'Do you have a problem serving my friend Mr Lee?'

The girl clutched her pad and pencil to her chest. 'Oh no, sir, Mr Lee is welcome here, it's just that we don't want no shootin'. This café is all my family has.'

Slack-faced, Toots asked, 'What are you talkin' about?'

Mr Schultz, the café's owner and girl's father, came from the kitchen. He leaned close. 'Please, Mr McGee, we heard about Danton and 'em other two. We don't want no shootin' in here.'

Murphy came into the café; he paused long enough to locate Toots and Chen, and then march to their table. 'It's good to see you up and around, Mr Lee.' Without giving Chen a chance to respond, he turned to Toots and asked, 'McGee?'

Toots nodded. 'You?'

'Murphy. I own the dry goods store.'

'What's goin' on?' asked Toots. 'Why's everybody spooked?'

Again, Murphy scanned the faces of the patrons. 'The words out, that you killed Danton and his men.'

'It was a fair enough fight,' Toots interrupted, 'considerin' it were three-to-one.'

'Hell, son. No one here cares a hoot about 'em. It's Griffin's new man, he's put the word around town that he's to know when you come into town. Bet he's already been told.'

'I still don't—'

Murphy talked over him. 'It's King Malone. Word is he's goin' to kill you on sight. You need to get out of town.'

'Oh,' said Toots, 'now I understand why everyone's so spooked.'

Chen said, 'You go back to the ranch, Toots, or at least you wait outside of town, and when I've finished at the dry goods store I'll follow.'

With a glance first at Murphy and the café owner, he looked at Chen. 'I've never run from a fight yet, and I don't plan to start today.' He smiled at Mr Schultz. 'I doubt Malone will rush in here guns blazin', so we'd like to order lunch.'

When it became clear that Toots planned to remain, the other patrons left money on their tables and hurried out. Soon, only Chen, Murphy, and Toots remained. 'We'll have the special, Mr Schultz. You care to join us, Mr Murphy?'

Murphy shook his head. 'I don't know if you're brave or

117

just a young fool, but I wish you luck. Mr Lee, see if you can talk some sense into him. Malone's a killer.' With that said, he took Chen's list of needed supplies and left the café.

Chen studied Toots for a long time. 'There is much about you that is not at first evident. You remained calm at the mention of Malone's name, yet all the others are afraid.'

A humorless smile came to Toots' face. 'I've faced men like him before.'

Schultz brought their food and moved to stand nervously by the café's door to watch while they ate. Chen's appetite was small; he pushed his food around and stared at Toots.

For his part, Toots relished the meal and asked for pie and coffee. When they'd finished eating, Toot's said, 'You go ahead to Murphy's. I'll be along after I settle the bill.'

Schultz stepped to the table his hands up palms out. 'There is no charge for the food. Just leave, please.'

'That's right neighborly of you, but it's not necessary.' Toots tossed two silver dollars on the table. 'I'd like more coffee while my friend here buys our supplies.'

Chen rose. 'The sooner I'm done the quicker we can leave. I'm sure Mr Murphy will see that I'm first to receive service.'

'Go ahead,' Toots could see Chen's reluctance to leave. 'I'll be along shortly.'

Chen turned and hurried from the café to Murphy's across the street. Toots stood with his coffee and watched. As Chen crossed the road's ridge between the worn ruts, Toots noticed a man dressed in black watching the café's door. It was King Malone.

Malone had positioned himself so that when they met, the sun, though high, would be in Toots's eyes. Toots turned to the café owner. 'Can I get out the back without being seen?'

118

At first, Schultz didn't seem to comprehend the question, and then his eyes lit up. 'Aw, yes you can get away through the rear door. You are smarter than I first thought. Come, it's this way.' Schultz led him through the kitchen out to an alleyway that duplicated the length of the street.

With a 'Thank you' said to Schultz, Toots followed the alley west for several buildings. Sure that he was behind Malone, Toots turned west for the main street. He peered around the corner of the building; Malone hadn't moved.

Toots pulled his Colt and slid a cartridge into the normally empty chamber. Now, he had six rounds. Without holstering his revolver, Toots stepped out on to the street and began walking north. The few citizens still on the street disappeared.

Malone saw men look past him and then dart into buildings. He glanced over his shoulder and saw the red-headed young man's approach. Like a big cat focused on its prey, he stalked down the center of the street. A flash of sunlight glinted off the nickel-plated revolver in McGee's hand; it gave him pause for concern.

He'd made sure that everyone around town knew he intended to gun down McGee on sight. McGee's immediate response direct and without evasion was unexpected. Well, I got to see this through, or. . . . He didn't have an alternative. He pulled his Colts; the familiar cool smoothness of their ivory grips gave him solace.

Malone willed his breathing to be slow, even and steady; he stepped out on to the street to wait. At thirty feet, the redhead halted. The town was dead silent, Malone's conversational toned voice carried well past Toots as Malone asked, 'McGee?'

Toots nodded.

119

'You the same McGee that was in Denver a while back?'

Again, Toots nodded.

The sun tracked across the southern sky east to west and was in his face, but McGee blocked most of it, so it wasn't much of an advantage. Then, as if McGee read his thoughts, the redhead moved to his left, which caused Malone's eyes to squint; the strain made his eyes water.

'We don't have to do this, Malone. Just take Griffin's money and ride away.'

Malone gave him a wry smile. 'You know how it is, McGee. Word gets around.'

'Yep, but you'd be alive. That's somethin' to think about.'

Somewhere in the back of his mind, it occurred to Malone that he might die today. There was something about the way McGee looked at him, almost as if he pitied him. This newfound knowledge brought a cold sinking feeling to his gut. It caused his intestines to cramp; it was fear. His palms began to sweat making them slippery; he milked the ivory gun butts trying to maintain a secure grip.

'How do you want to start the dance, Malone?'

Sweat trickled from his forehead and followed the creases of his pinched brow into his eyes. They burned; the tears blurred his vision. This is all wrong, how did this happen?

Malone's arms thrust up as he thumbed the Colts' hammers, but the handles twisted in his wet slippery palms. His shots went wild. The center of his chest burned; he gasped for air. Though his lungs filled, the breath had no value. Without blood surging through his veins, oxygen did not feed his muscles; he dropped his Colts – he no longer cared about them – and he clutched the clothes at his chest and pulled; the burning . . . he had to stop the burning.

Finally, relief came; the burning ceased and then he was cold, so cold. . . .

Malone crumpled to the dirt. A ringing in his ears was all that Toots heard for several seconds. Hands patted his back and then he heard people speaking. 'That was really somethin' – let me buy you a drink.' Another voice said, 'I'll be gone to hell; I never thought you stood a chance.' Then the crowd's voice became a noisy roar. From nowhere, Chen Lee stood beside him, and took him by the arm and led him away.

The crowd remained at Malone's body to take articles of his clothing, or cuts from his hair as mementos. By the time they reached the wagon, Toots had regained his senses. 'You've got sand, son. I'll give you that,' said Murphy. He and Chen had been in the doorway watching. 'That'll give Griffin cause to worry. Hot damn, son, I ain't never seen nothin' like it. You kilt King Malone. He's the deadliest gunman around.'

Murphy had filled Chen's order while he and Toots ate lunch, so Chen was ready to leave. 'Why not ride on the wagon with me.' Toots nodded and climbed up while Chen tied Knothead to the rear.

They were more than an hour down the trail, when Toots finally spoke. 'I wasn't sure I'd survive. I knew I could kill him, but there was a chance he'd get me too.' He paused for several seconds. 'Sarah doesn't need to know all the details.'

'If you wish, Toots, but she'd be proud to know that you're every bit the man her father was.'

Toots smiled. 'Those are some pretty big boots to fill.'

CHAPTER 13

Griffin stood at his office window watching the two men. It didn't bode well for Malone that McGee had gotten behind him, but. . . . His eyes blinked several times as he tried to grasp what had just happen. It was over; Malone lay dead in the street.

He clenched his teeth hard on his saliva-soaked cigar. The tobacco juice squirted across the back of his tongue, and trickled down his throat, souring his stomach.

As he stormed to his office, he told his clerk, 'I'll be gone for a few days, but don't say anythin' to anyone – understand?'

Griffin climbed the stairs to the private apartment he kept in town. He packed his saddle-bags and left town unnoticed.

Unshaven, wearing three days of travel debris, he didn't look like a prosperous businessman, so no one paid attention as he rode past Butte's fancy nice hotels for the red-light district. He reined up in front of the Montana Bell saloon. The owner, Christine Evans, was an old friend.

Inside, he looked around. Nothing much had changed, in fact, except for the girls, the place was the same. He selected a table near the stairway that led to the cribs above. Christine's room was up there too, but it was open to few.

It was early yet, and he was hungry. When the bartender came to his table, he said, 'Coffee and somethin' to eat.'

The bartender nodded. 'Beans and bacon good enough?' he asked.

'Good enough. Biscuits if you've got 'em.'

As the bartender left for the kitchen, Griffin tried to recall his name. It'd been close to five years since he'd been here, but still he should remember his name.

Griffin stared at him as he walked toward his table with a plate of food and a cup of hot coffee. The man was tall, his clothes hung from the bones of his shoulder. Clean shaven and a toothy grin. Tom Perry, that's his name.

'How have you been, Tom?'

The bartender hesitated for only a split second before he said. 'Fine, business is steady.'

'What time does Christine come down?'

This time Perry halted. He pinched his brow and took a hard look at Griffin as he place the order on the table. 'Do I know you?'

Griffin smiled. 'Think back a few years: less grey, thinner.'

A smile spread across Perry's face. 'Web Griffin, why I'll be damned. Heard you was up north.'

'Christine?'

Perry glanced at his pocket watch. 'She ought to be down anytime now. Want me to let her know you're here?'

'Nah, I'll surprise her.' Perry nodded and went to the bar.

The hot coffee was good; so was the food after three days of fixing his own grub. He was on his third cup when he heard footsteps above the bar. A glance confirmed it was Christine.

He watched her come down the stairs. His leering smile

revealed his thoughts. She's aged well. She wore a simmering green dress that accentuated her bosom; slit from ankle to mid-thigh it exposed her leg encased in a black net stocking.

She walked by his table. 'No hello for an old friend?'

When she turned, her smile was cold and impersonal. She took a few steps toward his table; her dark coffee-colored eyes peered at his face. His blue eyes twinkled below his bushy eyebrows. Her eyes widened with recognition. 'Web. Web, is that you?' As he stood, he gave her a toothy grin. 'It is you!'

Several quick steps closed the gap between them, and she flung her arms around his neck. He held her in his arms and whirled her around with a slap on her still firm bottom.

'It's good to see you, Christine.'

He put her down and held her at arm's length. She retained her figure; her hair now had streaks of grey, but it didn't distract from her youthful face.

She wrinkled her nose. 'You need a bath and a shave.' Turning to Tom, she said, 'Brandy, this requires a celebration.'

'None for me, Christine, but I wouldn't say no to the hospitality of your tub.'

A smile crossed her face. 'Sure, need your back washed?'

'Maybe,' he said. 'I might need other parts washed as well.'

'Tom, rouse that boy and get some hot water upstairs.'

'Yes, Christine,' said Tom and he left the barroom.

'Lie to me, tell me I'm the reason you're here.'

Griffin chuckled. 'There's that, but I need men, tough ones.'

Christine's lips pouted, but it wasn't genuine. 'Things aren't goin' well up north?'

His expression hardened; his voice held a harshness that wasn't customary between them. 'No,' he said. His tone shocked him, and he forced a smile. He exhaled with a sigh and sat back down feeling momentarily defeated. 'If I don't regain control of Charlo, I'll lose everythin'.'

She sat down beside him and took his hand. 'I know the gunmen in town. I'll send word for the best one and we'll meet with him tonight.'

A smile returned to his face. 'I'll have that brandy.'

Bathed and shaved, Griffin looked and felt his normal confident self. He sat with Christine at her private table sipping her brandy. Perry approached. 'Waco's here, says you sent for him.'

Her nod was curt. 'Send him over.'

Waco made his way to their table. Except for his revolvers, he looked like a cowboy. On his strong side, he carried a .44 Remington and his cross draw rig was a .44 LaMat grapeshot revolver.

The lean, clean-shaven man removed his hat as he approached and finger-combed black hair away from his intense blue eyes. 'You sent for me?' he asked Christine.

'Waco, this is Web Griffin. He's in need of' – she hesitated – 'your special services.'

Griffin stood; he gave the gunman a wry smile as Waco studied him. 'Sit down, Waco, I have a proposition for you.'

The gunman turned to Christine. 'You vouchin' for 'im?'

'Yes. I've known Web far a very long time.' She stood. 'I'll leave you two to talk business.'

Waco rounded the table and took her chair, which provided an unobstructed view of the entire room. 'What's your proposition?'

Griffin poured him a shot of brandy. 'I own land near

Charlo,' he began. Twenty minutes later Griffin finished. 'That's the fix I'm in. The sheriff won't be a problem, but there's a federal judge I need to get out of town. While the judge and I are gone, I want you and a dozen men to wipe out the Baxter ranch.'

'How many at the ranch?' Waco asked.

'Including the two women and a Chinaman: ten. Are the women going to be a problem for you?'

Waco shook his head. 'Not if the money's right.'

'I'll give you five thousand dollars for the job. I want it to look like a band of raiders. You, or it, can't be traced back to me. Got that?'

The gunman gave him a single nod.

'All right then, I'll pay you half now and leave the other half here with Christine. She'll get a telegram from me tellin' her to pay you when you're finished.'

A sneer crossed Waco's face. 'You know what'll happen if you try to cross me.'

Griffin met Waco's stare. 'That goes both ways.'

Waco sat back in his chair, his shoulders lowered and his face held an almost pleasant expression. 'How long do I have to get it done?'

'I leave in the morning. Allow a week for travel and time to arrange things with Judge Miller.' Griffin paused again. 'Let's see, another week to return to Butte and schedule a meeting with Govern. . . .' He'd been thinking aloud. Finished, he turned to Waco. 'You need to strike fourteen days from tomorrow at the soonest and eighteen days at the latest.'

Toots saw Big Mose point toward the ridge. He looked and could just make out a buckboard and accompanying riders. It would take thirty minutes or more before they reached the house; he finished his chore. Then he joined Helen and

Sarah on the porch as the wagon drew closer; it was John Roberts from the Rocking-R.

'Howdy, Mr Roberts,' called Toots as he stepped down from the porch to greet the old rancher.

'Hullo there,' Roberts answered back. When the buckboard reined in, Toots played out the lead and tied it to the porch.

Helen stood at the edge of the porch. 'Won't you please come in for coffee and pie? I've something a bit stronger if you like.'

The old man stood and stretched his back and limbered his knees before he climbed down from the wagon. 'I'm gettin' too old for a horse. One of these days soon, I'll be ridin' in the back on my way to the bone yard.'

'Why, no such thing, Mr Roberts,' said Helen, 'you look the same as when we first met.'

A twinkle came to his eyes. 'Did I truly look that bad?'

'Of course not! That's not what I meant at all.' Helen was flustered.

Robert chuckled. 'I knowed what you meant, Mrs Baxter. I was just funnin'.'

She smiled, but it didn't reflect any humor. Roberts followed Helen and Sarah into the house, while Toots showed the men to the bunkhouse and the corral for their horses.

When Toots came through the kitchen's rear door, he found Mr Roberts sipping hot coffee and eating left over biscuits stuffed with slices of cold bacon.

'What brings you to the ranch?' asked Helen.

'Rumors. I been hearin' tales about young McGee here and wanted find out if they was true.'

Everyone turned to stare at Toots, which caused his cheeks to pink. 'Not sure what you're talkin' about, Mr Roberts.'

The twinkle returned to Robert's eyes and his lips curled at the corners. 'Why I hear tell that you've buffaloed the sheriff and shot it out with King Malone.'

'Who is King Malone?' asked Helen.

Roberts relished the question. 'Why, he was the meanest killer in the territory, and McGee here met 'im on the streets of Charlo and killed 'im in a fair fight.' He looked from Helen to Sarah. Both were wide-eyed and pale. 'You mean you didn't know?' he asked.

Toots glanced at Sarah, who was over the shock of hearing such news. Her eyes were now squinted and a thin line replaced her mouth. Hands to her hips, she stepped closer to him. 'Just when were you going to tell me about this?'

He looked to Chen for help, but the Chinaman turned back to the stove and fussed with the coffee pot. 'It weren't like Mr Roberts said. It was sort of—'

'Toussaint William McGee, you killed a professional gunman in the streets of Charlo. Just how was it, "sort of"?'

Helen came to his aid. 'Sarah, we have a guest.'

Sarah returned her attention to Mr Roberts. 'Is there anything we ought to know?'

Roberts's grin couldn't have been larger. 'Sorry, son, I didn't mean to get you into hot water.' He glanced at Sarah. 'No, missy, there's nothin' else, but I'd say what he's done is plenty.'

Toots, eager to change the subject asked, 'You said you was goin' down to Butte, Mr Roberts?'

He sipped his coffee. 'Rustlin's started up over to my place. Knowin' what's happened to you folks, well I figure Griffin's got somethin' to do with it. Goin' down to see Potts an' get a federal marshal up here or may be the Army to investigate. If we're to become part of the union then we got to have law-n-order.'

'I wish you more success with him than I had,' said Helen.

'I got letters from several of the other large ranchers. I don't think he'll want us complainin' to Washington about his not doin' his job.'

Helen smiled, her cheeks rose, and her eyes became twinkling crescents. 'Benjamin is a politician if nothing else. I'm sure you'll have his full attention, Mr Roberts.'

'Please call me John. I'd prefer that if you would.'

'If you wish, John, but you must call me Helen.' There was a pause. Helen said, 'You'll stay for supper and we'll put you up for the night.'

'It's not necessary, Helen. We was plannin' to spend the night in Charlo. Movin' on early in the mornin'.'

'Oh, please reconsider, John. Visitors are so infrequent.'

Roberts grinned. 'Well, I don't want you to think me rude.'

Later, on the porch, Sarah confronted Toots. 'I talked to Chen,' she said wringing her hands as she spoke. 'He said you had a chance to leave town without havin' a showdown with Malone. Why didn't you leave? You could've been killed. Aren't I important to you?'

As she waited for him to reply, she bit her lower lip between her teeth and looked up at him with glistening chestnut-colored eyes. His heart ached with the fact that he caused her to worry. 'Sarah, I'd never do anythin' on purpose to hurt you. I hope you know that. It was on account of you that I faced Malone. He was Griffin's new ringer intent on killin' me one way or another.'

Sarah stepped in close and embraced Toots. Her head against his chest, she sighed. 'But you could've been killed.'

He stroked her hair. 'True enough, but I took the fight to 'im on my terms. The advantage was mine.'

Roberts and Helen came out on the porch. 'I like a good

smoke before I turn in for the night. How about you, McGee?'

'No, sir, I never started the habit. Seemed a waste of money to me.'

Roberts stiffened slightly, but then relaxed his shoulders and laughed. 'So it is, young man, so it is.'

Helen, who carried a tray, sat it a table near the rockers. 'What's your thought about fine brandy, William?' she asked.

'Well ma'am – Helen – I don't want you to think me rude. . . .'

Laughter drifted across the valley.

At first light the next morning Roberts and his men again were on the trail headed for Butte with the addition of a letter to Benjamin Potts from Helen Baxter. Late morning found them south of Charlo, where they encountered Griffin. Trail clothes and debris disguised Griffin to a point that Roberts, at first, didn't know him. It was Griffin's eyes that Roberts recognized.

Roberts reined back. 'Whoa,' said Roberts and squinted at the rider's face. 'Griffin, what the hell you doin' out here?'

Griffin didn't break his mount's stride. 'Mind your own business, Roberts.' He sneered, heeled his horse and galloped away.

Roberts turned to watch him ride away. Aloud, he said, 'What the devil was that all about?'

He pondered what he saw. He must've been down to Butte to speak to the governor. Well, I have some things to say to Potts; we'll see what's what.

In the anteroom of Potts's office, Roberts paced the floor.

He'd been there for over an hour and his patience was nearly gone. He stepped to the clerk's desk and asked, 'Who's in there with Potts?'

The clerk looked up with a surprised expression. 'Why no one. The governor is reviewing important documents.'

'Why, that mealy-mouthed son-of-a-bitch,' said Roberts, and he pulled on his hat, situated his gun-belt and marched towards Potts' office door.

'Sir,' called the clerk. 'You have to wait until the governor is ready to see you.'

Roberts yanked his Remington from its holster and shot a hole in the clerk's desk. The clerk jumped back, and Roberts shot a hole in the floor at the clerk's feet. The clerk's eyes went wide; he clasped his hands to his chest, and a large dark circle formed at his crotch.

Potts, who remained at his desk, jerked his hands into the air when Roberts stormed into his office. Roberts had not holstered his lead slinger.

'Mr Roberts, what's the problem?' asked Potts.

'You've left me coolin' my heels out there for the better part of an hour. Who the hell do you thin' you are. Hell, I can get into Grant's office quicker.'

'I'm sorry, John. My clerk didn't tell me that you were waiting. Had I known, you'd have been shown right in. Please accept my apologies. I'll have a word with the clerk. It won't happen again.'

Roberts held up his revolver. 'I believe he'll remember who I am should I need to see you in the future.' His words struck his sense of humor and he began to laugh. 'The little piss-ant wet his self. Ain't he ever heard a gunshot afore?'

Potts put his hands down and began to shuffle the papers on his desk. He gave Roberts a forced smile. 'We've begun to see civilization come to Montana. The discharge of

131

firearms inside town limits has become a rare occurrence. Now, what is it that I can do for you, John?'

Robert's expression became somber, and he stood erect at the front of Potts's desk. 'I don't know what kind of deal you and Griffin have goin', but it stops today.'

Potts jerked back in his chair as if he'd been slapped, his mouth worked but nothing came out. Red-faced, he rose to his feet. 'You're accusing me of being in cahoots with Griffin? Why, I'll have you—'

'Potts,' said Roberts. 'I ran into Griffin returning from Butte. Who else but you would he be seein'?'

The governor came around his desk and got face to face with Roberts. 'He damn well didn't see me. You can check my clerk's records.'

Roberts pulled the letters from his pocket. 'Griffin is runnin' a crooked operation from Charlo. Mrs Baxter delivered her complaint in person. I'm givin' you mine and here are letters from the other large ranches near mine.' He tossed the letters on the Governor's desk. 'What are you goin' to do about it?'

Potts's opened mouth snapped shut and he stepped back from Roberts; pulled at his starched collar, and smoothed the front of his pinstriped suit. His eyes dropped down at the stack of letters on his desk.

'John, I promise you, I had no idea about Griffin. I thought Helen Baxter's complaints were more about her husband's death than anything else, trying to place blame. . . .'

'There's a letter from her too. It says she got proof and with it, she's got my vote,' Roberts was still angry. 'Griffin killed her husband and son sure as I'm standin' here. What're you goin' to do about that?'

Potts collapsed into his chair, and looked up at Roberts

with despair. 'I'll have one of the deputy marshals come up there and start an investigation.'

'Goddamn it, Potts,' said Roberts, his face color grew from red to purple. 'That's too little too late. You need to get the Army up there now.'

'John, I can't—'

'You get the Army up there now or,' he glanced at the letters, 'we'll contact our friends in Washington.'

Potts's shoulders fell. 'All right, John, you win. It'll take a couple of days, but they'll be there.'

CHAPTER 14

Griffin paced to and fro in front of his office window. He searched his mind for the words to win his argument. 'Judge, I tell you this is our only reasonable option. Hollister can't deal with this McGee fellow, and if we go out there with anythin' less than the Army—'

'—but why do we have to go to Butte? I can send the governor a telegram. I'm sure he'll—'

'Damn it, Judge.' Griffin's face reddened with his agitation at the judge's continued resistance to accompanying him to Butte. 'You know Potts. He won't do anything unless someone lights a fire under him. Without us bein' there to explain, he'll just put it off.'

Judge Miller sighed. 'All right, I'll go, but I still think it's a needless waste of time.'

Griffin stopped pacing and exhaled deeply, he felt the tension in his muscles release. He smiled at the judge. 'I would hate to have to argue a case in front of your court, Judge.'

Miller returned the smile. 'Oh, I don't know. You'd probably do all right. You're persistent, that's what counts.'

'Can you be ready to catch the morning stage?' asked Griffin.

The judge grimaced. 'If I must.' He stood to leave. 'If I'm

going down there, I've some other matters that need my attention. I have some paperwork to deal with. You'll have to excuse me, Web. See you in the morning.'

Toots sat with Sarah, Helen, and Chen around the kitchen table. 'I know that it's been quiet since that business in town,' said Toots, in answer to Helen's suggestion that their troubles were over, 'but that's just it – I can't see Griffin quittin' without a reason.'

'I support Toots's thinking, Mrs Baxter,' said Chen. 'He will try something else. What that might be I can't imagine.'

'My bet is that he'll go for broke,' said Toots. 'And that makes 'im more dangerous 'an a wounded mountain lion.'

Sarah asked, 'What can we do?'

Toots looked at her and saw the wistfulness in her eyes. 'All we can do is stay on guard. He'll try somethin', I'm sure of it.'

'We can't wait for ever, William,' said Helen. 'We need to buy stock and return this ranch to a profitable operation.'

'I been thinkin' on that, Helen,' said Toots. 'Accordin' to Danton, there are some of our stock bein' held a-ways up in the mountains. Soon as this is settled, I figured on findin' 'em.'

'We have additional funds, Mrs Baxter,' said Chen. 'You needn't worry.'

Helen massaged her brow. 'I just want this mess to be over, so we can go back to our lives. Is that too much to ask?'

'No, Mama, it's not.' Sarah put her arm around her mother's shoulder. 'It'll be over soon. I just know it will.'

Toots and Chen exchanged glances; they weren't so sure.

The next day, Toots began scouting the countryside much the same way Sarah had done when he first arrived. Griffin was up to something, but he just couldn't put his figure on what it was.

On the third day of scouting, he smelled smoke a-ways to the south. It's midday, why a fire? Rustlers?

He rode slow, following a game trail that led in the same general direction. After an hour's tedious travel, he heard voices and other camp noises. He eased out of the saddle. After ground-hitching Knothead, he removed his spurs and put them into his saddle-bags. Quiet as possible, he levered a round into his Winchester's chamber and set off in the direction of the noise.

Soon, the sounds were distinguishable; the clink of a metal cup, the clunk of wood being stacked, or the jingle of spurs. Toots gauged the distance as close, and glanced about for a tree he could climb. He hid his rifle, and scurried up a tall pine.

His elevation from the tree gave him a view of their entire camp. They were a rough bunch of men, who – except for the quality of their weapons, and the way they handled them – could be cowboys like him. One man, who sat away from the others, sipped coffee and studied a diagram he'd drawn in the dirt.

'Hey, Waco, you want some grub?' asked the bearded man tending the pots on the fire.

The man turned away from his diagram, and said, 'Yeah, some more coffee too.'

Toots scrutinized the man they called Waco. *Could that be Waco Turner from Texas? I'd heard he'd come north an' hired out his gun to settle range wars. What's he doin' here?* The answer seemed to be self-evident. *He's on Griffin's payroll. I wonder what they're waiting for.*

His time spent concealed in the tree yielded its reward. A sluggish man in ill-fitted clothes finished his meal and, after scraping his plate, turned to Waco. 'What're we waitin' fer? There's not that many, let's just kill 'em and move on.'

Waco shook his head. 'How many times I got to tell you. The man payin' the bill has to be in Butte for his alibi. Then we can go. The soonest is day after tomorrow.'

'Two days,' whispered Toots, and then he shimmed down the tree and made his way back to Knothead. He smiled at his horse. Many a cowboy has had a long walk home thinking their animal would wait with just their reins hanging loose on the ground.

Everyone, including Helen and Sarah, was in the bunkhouse.

'That's what I heard 'em say. Soon as Griffin's had time to make it to Butte, they attack.'

'How we goin' to play it, Boss?' asked Little Mose.

Toots stroked his face and was surprised to find it smooth. He glanced at Sarah and gave her a smile, which she returned with an understanding wink. *Damn ain't she shameless. . . .*

'Boss?' prompted Little Mose.

Color rose up Toots's neck as he realized that his mind had been elsewhere. They all turned to stare at Sarah when she started to giggle, which made it worse for Toots.

'Ahem,' said Toots, and their attention returned to him. He feigned as if nothing had interrupted them. 'They've got us out gunned near two-to-one.' He paused to let the odds sink in. 'Waco's the key. If we can get 'im the rest'll move on.'

'So how do we get 'im?' asked Big Nose Karl. 'We goin' to sneak out there and ambush 'em while they's asleep?'

Toots glanced at Helen. Her posture was ramrod straight and he saw the muscles ripple on her jaw, but she didn't dissent from the suggestion. *She's got grit*, thought Toots.

'I thought about that, Karl, but that'd be cold-blooded murder. It ain't right.'

137

'But,' Karl objected, 'that's what they got planned for us.'

Slight curls formed at the corners of Toots's mouth. 'If they do and get caught they'll hang. Is that what you want for us?'

Karl pulled in his horns with an 'Aw'; he didn't finish his words when he saw that Helen stared at him.

'Here's my plan,' said Toots as he glanced up to make sure everyone listened. 'If we include Mrs Baxter and Sarah we've got ten guns. I want to set a trap here at the ranch. We know when they'll come. The surprise will be on them. Karl, if you're willing' – Karl nodded – 'we'll be up on the ridge line while you all wait for 'em down here. Once the shootin' starts, we'll attack them from their rear. We'll focus on gettin' Waco.'

'Won't they get suspicious with us holed up here?' ask Gus.

'There's cover for daylight attack,' said Toots. 'So they'll have to attack just before dawn. They'd expect us to be in our beds and, by the time we got to our guns, it'd be over and done.'

All the next day, every man was armed regardless of his chore; even Chen had his carbine propped next to the kitchen door. Toots sat with Helen and Sarah sipping coffee. 'What do you think of our chances, William?' asked Helen.

With a smile meant to show confidence, a boyish grin of delighted anticipation developed. 'I believe we've a better chance 'an Waco and his boys. After the first shot, they won't know what hit 'em.'

Strangely enough, the smile and his words seemed to bolster their spirits.

'We'll certainly do our part,' said Helen, her face solemn with resolve.

It was 2 a.m. when Gus shook Toots's shoulder. 'It's time. Karl's in the barn waiting with your pony.'

Despite his restlessness earlier, he'd fallen asleep and now had difficulty waking. It was a moonless night, but Toots knew his way about the bunkhouse. He moved to the stove with the aid of starlight, squinted to see if the coffee pot was there. 'No coffee, huh?' he asked, disappointment in his voice.

After a long cat-like stretch, he pulled on his boots, strapped on his Colt, and headed for the barn. He was careful to stay in the shadow of the bunkhouse just in case Waco watched.

Inside the barn, he found Karl waiting with Knothead saddled and ready to go. To his pleasant surprise, in the shielded light from a candle, he saw that Sarah and Chen were there also. Sarah came to see him off and wish him good luck; Chen brought biscuits with cold bacon and coffee.

Toots's eyes gleamed with desire as he stared at the coffee and biscuits. 'Well,' said Sarah with a huff, 'I believe you're happier to see Chen 'an me.'

He altered his approach towards Chen, and stepped to Sarah and embraced her. 'Now, you know that ain't true. It's just that I ain't had time to shave.'

Sarah gave in to his embrace and kissed him, her lips wet with passion and desire. Still in his embrace, she leaned back and put a hand to his face. 'I'll forgive you this once, but don't think you can make a habit of not shavin'.'

'Yes, ma'am,' he said and released her and immediately turned back to Chen, who'd already poured his coffee.

'Thank you, Chen. I surely need this, this mornin'. I'll need all my wits later and without this. . . .' He gulped down the cooled cup and held out the empty cup for more.

Chen said, 'I've put food in your saddle-bags. I wanted to wish you and Mr Karl good hunting.' He bowed slightly.

Feeling a bit awkward, Toots, with a cup in one hand and a biscuit in the other, returned the bow. Chen, who seemed amused by his gesture, smiled.

They led their horses through the man-door at the rear of the barn. Outside, they rode north to the far side of the lake and from there westward with the tree line to conceal their silhouettes. Concealed between the tall pines, they waited. In a whispered voice Karl asked, 'How do we play this?'

'We'll wait until they pass and fall in behind 'em. When the shootin' starts, we'll light from our saddles and let 'em have it from ground cover with our rifles.'

The sky lighted to a dark smoky-grey, but visibility without the moon's light remained poor. They heard Waco's approach several minutes before they could make out their silhouettes. Waco and his men formed a line atop the ridge that paralleled the valley.

Toots heard Waco's voice.

He's at the center, he thought. *They've formed a line like the cavalry, aimed on makin' a charge.*

Waco led off at a walk. His men, though the line was ragged, kept pace. Soon they spurred their animals to a gallop, and Toots and Karl left the trees in pursuit.

His timing was perfect. The morning light outlined ranch buildings, but the sun was not yet high enough to be in their eyes. 'This'll be like shootin' fish in a barrel. Let's get to it, boys.'

As prearranged, Waco and four men broke right toward the house. The remainder made for the bunkhouse. *Strange,* thought Waco, *there's no response to our approach. Have they pulled out?*

Only after the muzzle flash from the barn's loft and the crack of rifle fire did it occur to him that the silence meant that it could be a trap. The fusillade emptied saddles like skittles falling in a game of ten-pins. Waco spurred his mount and bolted to the south leaving his men to face their circumstances. With a glance over his shoulder, he saw two of his men, who had attacked the bunkhouse, veer north, and without looking back rode hell bent for leather.

Toots and Karl saw the muzzle flash from the barn. They slid their mounts to a halt, and with long guns in hand, they bailed from their saddles and threw themselves to the ground in time to watch the carnage.

The sun crested the house's roof and shone its light on the bloodshed; ten men lay dead or dying. Four of the ten horses were down, the remainder fidgeted against their hanging reins.

Toots and Karl rose and walked among the fallen; two still lived but had no chance of surviving. Toots looked down at one. 'You're gut shot,' he said without a hint of pity in his voice.

The man grimaced. 'I figured. You got my spine too; I can't move or feel nothin' from the waist down. Go ahead an' finish me.'

'It's not my call,' said Toots. He retrieved the man's fallen revolver and emptied the cylinder, and then replaced one cartridge. He tossed the gun on the ground and used the toe of his boot to nudge it close to the man's hand. 'You takes your chances, you gots to pay when you lose.'

The man gripped his revolver. 'I could shoot you.'

Toots gave the man a wry smile. 'You've got one bullet in that shooter; feel free to use it how you think best.' He turned and walked away. Part way to the house, he heard the gun's report; he paused and walked on.

Sarah ran out of the house and threw herself into his

arms. 'Toots, I was so afraid. Are you hurt?'

He held her close; her smell comforted and aroused him. When his manhood responded, Sarah started and pulled away from him. For once, he didn't blush, but rather he stared at her, his flames of desire raged in his gaze. She flushed and paused but for a moment, and again threw herself at him; their kisses were deep and made them hunger.

A gunshot broke their embrace; Karl shot a wounded horse. They parted and looked at one another, as their passion subsided, nervous laughter followed. Helen, Chen, Gus and the others came out to the yard to see the results of their handiwork.

Helen said, 'My God, we've killed so many.' She looked at their faces. 'Some of them are so young.'

Sarah went to her mother's side and put her arm around her to comfort and support her. 'They attacked us, Mama. If it wasn't for William and the men, we'd be dead.'

'I suppose you're right, Sarah, but it still seems such a waste.' Arm-in-arm, they returned to the house.

Gus walked over to Toots, and asked, 'Now what?'

Toots took his eyes off Sarah and her mother. 'Anybody hurt?'

'Nope,' said Gus. 'It couldn't have gone better. 'Them sons-of-bitches didn't know what hit 'em.' He chuckled. 'Guess we ought to plant 'em.'

'Yeah,' said Toots, 'but not near here. Take 'em off toward the tree line and turn a spade over 'em there.' Gus nodded and signaled to the men, who went to gather the wagon and necessary tools.

At the house, Chen had waited in the kitchen. They gathered there, and he poured generous glasses of brandy; they drank in silence. After a while, Helen asked, 'What's next?'

Toots sat at the table, weary from the lack of sleep and the tension of the battle. Thinking aloud, he said, 'We missed Waco and two more that headed north.' He paused to sip the brandy, but sat it down on the table. 'Chen, I'd rather have coffee if there is any.'

Chen nodded and turned to the stove. 'I'm learning to have a fresh pot brewing when you're around, Toots.'

'Please just call me William like Helen and Sarah do.'

'If you like, William.'

Sarah interrupted. 'You were saying that two men rode north?'

Toots's stare was blank, then he recalled. 'I could be wrong, but my money's bettin' we've seen the last of 'em. Waco's another question. He's got a reputation to keep up, so there's a good chance we haven't seen the last of him.'

Waco veered westward at a dead run toward the tree line. Cresting the ridge, he hauled back on the reins, sliding his horse to a halt. With a tight grip on his Henry, he stepped out of the saddle and snatched the glasses from his saddle-bag.

He lay on the ridge top and scanned the valley; there was no pursuit. Fingers on the focal knob, he adjusted the binoculars to watch the house. He could see McGee's red hair. 'This isn't over, McGee,' he muttered.

The rush of adrenaline and the hard ride of the escape left him exhausted; he lay his head on his crossed arms and slept. The sun was high when he woke with a start; his horse whinnied.

Waco looked around; he saw cows milling about the ridgeline. As yet, they were unattended, but that would change. He led his horse down the ridge several yards before mounting; he skulked away into the trees.

CHAPTER 15

'The governor will see you now, gentlemen.' Griffin and Judge Miller rose and strolled into Potts's office. Griffin noted Potts didn't rise or offer a greeting. When the door closed, Potts said, 'God damn it, Griffin, what the hell you been doing up there?'

Incensed, Griffin came out of his seat. 'What do you mean? I told you I needed the Army to settle things in Charlo. That Baxter woman has hired gunfighters and I can't enforce the eviction notice without soldiers.'

'The Army will be there within the week,' said Potts. Griffin began to smile, but stopped when he saw the sneer on Potts' face. 'But they'll be after your hide, not Helen Baxter's.'

'What are you talkin' about, Potts?' asked Griffin.

Judge Miller looked uneasy. As he stood, he said, 'If you'll excuse me, I'll leave you two to resolve your issues.'

'Not so fast, Miller,' said Potts. 'You're part of this. Sit!'

Miller puffed up. 'I'm a federal judge appointed by President Grant. You can't talk to me that way.'

Potts's eyes narrowed as he leaned forward to stare at the judge. 'A telegram from me to Grant will get you un-appointed, now sit.' Miller dropped back into his chair.

Griffin wasn't sure why, but he followed Miller's example and sat down.

Potts rose and paced the floor behind his desk. 'Listen to me carefully. John Roberts was in this office three days ago, and he left a pile of letters from the other ranchers accusing you of rustling and murder. One of the letters was from Helen Baxter, who claims to have a signed confession—'

Griffin interrupted. 'She can't prove anything. Danton's dead, killed by her gunman McGee.'

Potts took a deep breath as he tried to curb his boiling anger, but he still glared at Griffin. 'The confession is from Sheriff Hollister.'

Griffin's jaw slacked and his mouth fell open. 'What?' he asked. 'What are you talkin' about? Hollister's out of town. I can get this cleared up as soon as I return. I need the Army.'

Potts stared at Griffin for the longest time. At length, he spoke, his tone softer even consolatory as he explained. 'Listen to me, Web. The territory is soon to become a state. Law and order must prevail or it will never happen. Do you understand what I'm saying?' Griffin looked bewildered. Potts sighed and continued. 'I've allowed you great latitude with regards to your business dealings, but you've gone too far. Other men of importance now stand against you.'

His face reddened and he glared at Potts. 'Give me their names an' I'll deal with 'em.'

Potts shook his head and looked to Miller for help.

Miller said, 'Web, you must listen to the governor. He knows best.'

Griffin turned on Miller, his stare maniacal. 'You're both yellow, lowdown-lily-livered cowards. Why, I bet you'd both shit yourselves before you'd fight—'

'That's enough, Web,' snapped Judge Miller.

Potts added, 'It's no good, Web. If a word about this gets

145

back East, we'll lose statehood, and I'll be recalled.'

'Benjamin, we've been friends a long time. OK, you can't send the Army to help me, but you can hold off a few days. All I need is a little time and I'll have everything worked out. I promise the people of Charlo will not say a word. In return, I'll give you and Miller ten percent of my holdings – you'll be filthy rich. Grant and the others can go hang themselves.'

Potts looked to Miller, who shrugged. 'Forty percent, Web. After all, if you fail then it's forty percent of nothing.'

Griffin smiled. He had them, but not at forty percent. 'Twenty five.'

Again, Potts and Miller exchanged glances but this time there was a perceptible nod from the judge. Potts said, 'Agreed. Miller will draft a contract while we wait.'

Griffin stayed with Christine after his dealings with the governor and Miller. It'd been four days and still no word from Waco. He sat at Christine's table sipping her fine brandy when a trail-weary rider entered the saloon from the alleyway door. Engrossed with their conversation, they didn't notice his presence until he stood at the side of their table.

They looked up. 'Waco,' said Griffin, excitement in his voice. 'Tell me, is it done?'

The killer sneered at Griffin with a menacing stare. 'I ought to kill you where you sit. I want the rest of my money.'

Griffin's brow pinched with confusion, but he didn't cower. 'Have you lost your mind? What are you talking about?'

'It was a trap. They ambushed us when we rode in and I lost ten men, maybe more.'

Griffin exhaled with a frustrated sigh that bordered on a growl. *My plans depended on Waco's success; now what?*

'I said I want the rest of my money—'

The enraged Griffin tossed his brandy into Waco's face, and then slammed his fist into the gunman's stomach. Doubled over, Waco stumbled back, but Griffin was out of his chair and on him. He grabbed a handfull of Waco's hair keeping him bent and brought up his knee into his face, which reared him backward, allowing Griffin to slam him to the floor.

Blinded by alcohol, Waco reached for his gun. Griffin stomped his wrist, drew, and thrust his Derringer under Waco's chin.

'Shoot if you're going to or let me up.'

Griffin collected Waco's weapons and handed them to Christine. 'Tom,' he called to the bartender, 'fresh glasses.'

'What about my money?' asked Waco.

'If you were as persistent with completing the job I assigned you, you'd be paid. I don't owe you anything. However, if you want to try again I'll pay you $5,000 – interested?'

Waco perked up. 'Go on, I'm listenin'.'

As Griffin considered, he absently looked away and pulled on his left ear. Several minutes passed; he looked up and said, 'I want thirty men who will kill, no questions asked. How long to recruit them and how much a head?'

Weeks went by, and people fell into a routine similar to their old way of living; Chen and Toots went to Charlo several times. The townsfolk were friendly, going out of their way to shake Toots's hand. Griffin had not been seen, though his clerk kept his office opened for business. Hollister was also missing. Toots secretly assumed that the lawman took his advice and went back east to find a tamer life.

Men began drifting to the ranch looking for work. When the crew counted twelve men, Toots decided it was time to ride north and search for the rustled Box-B cattle. With Helen's blessing, he left Gus in charge.

After grub the next morning, Toots led Big Nose Karl and five hands north from the ranch. Karl lived with the Crow in his earlier days, and he learned how to track; furthermore, he was more than familiar with the countryside.

Karl scanned the landscape. 'It's been a good while since they was took. Ain't no sign left.' He stood in his stirrups to study the terrain. 'You figure they come this way?'

'That's what Danton claimed,' said Toots.

He settled back into his saddle. 'There's grass and water in the canyon lands north of here,' said Karl. He rubbed the back of his neck. 'I ain't so sure about it though – the water's steady, but the grass is sparse. If they're there then they got to be mostly bones by now.'

'Well, Karl, we got to find 'em first to see.'

Karl led the group as they loped away northward.

Roberts forked his horse on a hilltop overlooking the south range. He didn't ride much anymore because of the pain to his hip joint; on good days, however, when the distance was short, he saddled the roan. Today, he watched his men branding strays.

A bearded, rough-looking man approached him. Roberts noted his ascent of the hill several minutes earlier and waited. 'What'd you find out, O'Malley?' asked Roberts.

O'Malley gave Roberts a large toothy grin that belayed his tough appearance. 'I done like you told me, Boss. I hung around, kept my mouth shut, and my eyes open. Sure enough, a few days after you left Griffin was in town. He met up with Waco Turner. They're hirin' men for gun work.'

Roberts's brow hooded his eyes, his jaw clenched, and through his teeth he asked, 'What's the job?'

'It's the Box-B, Boss.' O'Malley paused again. 'I figure they'll hit 'em in the next two or three days.'

'Did you find out how many?'

O'Malley smiled. 'Yes, sir, they was tryin' to recruit thirty men. They was most full up when I talked to 'em.'

'Good job, O'Malley. Now here's what I want you to do. . . .'

It was close to noon; Roberts and three of his neighbors sat in his parlor. 'Thank you for coming on such short notice, gentlemen,' said Roberts. 'I've got news and I think a chance to put a nail in Griffin's coffin.'

They muttered. Finally, Jack Spooner, a man near Roberts's age and appearance, said, 'Out with it.'

Ben Warren, the youngest, who owned the smallest ranch of the four, said, 'Just tell us what you need for us to do, Mr Roberts.'

Jeremy Updike, the Brit, nodded for him to proceed.

'Potts sided with us,' Roberts began. 'He's left Griffin to deal on his own.'

Several minutes passed as he explained the situation. '—so I figured we'd get involved. Between the four of us, we ought to be able to field forty to fifty men. Are you with me?'

Spooner spoke first. 'I can't order my men to go with you, but I'll talk to 'em and let any of 'em who want go along.'

'I ain't as big as you three,' said Warren, 'but my hands an' me'll ride.'

Updike listened to each man, and only after all were staring at him, did he speak. 'Who will command this expedition?'

Spooner shrugged. 'I'm too old for a ruckus on horseback.' He glanced at Roberts.

'I'm goin',' said Roberts, 'but I'm afraid I'm with Jack

when it comes to forkin' a horse. I sort of thought we'd let young Mr McGee do the honors. He's been doin' pretty fair so far.'

Warren said, 'That's fine by me.'

Updike added, 'From what you've told me, this McGee should be able to handle the affair, and like you gentlemen, I too shall go along. I wish to see that my interests are assured.'

Roberts beamed with satisfaction. 'It's a might early, but I got some smooth whiskey from Canada.'

Spooner grinned. 'Hell, yes. It's good for the snakebite problem in my back.'

'Just one,' said Warren. 'I got lots to do before I leave.'

Updike stepped to the desk where the whiskey bottles stood. 'Be a good fella won't you. Pour mine into a tall glass.'

'Aw hell, make 'em all tall,' said Spooner. 'I may be gettin' too old for some things, but not good whiskey.'

Roberts held up his glass. 'Here's to our success and Griffin's bust.'

They had agreed to meet on the Charlo road after their breakfasts the next morning. The final count including the ranch owners was forty-eight men. Spooner, Warren, and Updike led the column. Next was Roberts, driving a wagon full of ammunition and other supplies; the remaining forty-four men rode two abreast like a column of cavalry.

Griffin's men gathered five miles north of Butte. He had thirty men, led by Waco Turner, and four packhorses with supplies for the trip cross-country to the Box-B.

They were a surly lot, but all were afraid of Waco's fast gun and willingness to use it, so they followed Griffin's orders. Each night, Griffin reviewed his map of the Box-B and surrounding areas.

'I've been thinkin', Waco,' said Griffin. 'They must have been patrollin' the valley and found you out. So, we'll send two men ahead to scout the valley when we're closer. The last night's camp will be cold and we'll hit at sun-up from the southeast – here.' He poked at the map.

'The men ain't goin' to like that, Griffin.'

'Would they rather be killed instead? I mean to finish this thing once and for all.'

Waco nodded. 'I'll deal with 'em.' He turned to scan the group of men. 'We don't need to send more 'an one man to scout the valley though. Red Shirt over there is Comanche. I rode with him in Texas. He'll do the job right enough.'

'If you vouch for 'em, I'll go along with the choice. Let's get movin'. We're wastin' time.'

Waco walked over to Red Shirt. 'Red Shirt, scout ahead, markin' the trail for us. When you're close to the valley check it out and report back to me. We don't want no surprises.'

Red Shirt nodded, swung on to his pony, and rode out of camp.

Everyone was on their feet watchin'. Waco said, 'Mount up, we're movin' out.'

Griffin joined him, and they rode in the direction Red Shirt led. He wore a smile, for the first time in weeks – the excited feeling, the anticipation of winning returned.

The last night before the attack and the men grumbled about not having fires and hot food. Finally, Waco had enough. 'You men act like dudes, the whole lot of you. You've had cold camps afore.' He looked around for a dissenter, but no one spoke up. 'All right then, stop your grumblin'. Tomorrow, we hit the Bar-B ranch. You get paid your hundred dollars, and you're on your own.'

It was full dark, with only a crescent moon and the stars

for light, when Red Shirt returned to camp. To Waco, he said, 'Seven men with the cook and two women. Late in the day, four men with wagon of supplies come: two old, two young.'

'Good work, Red Shirt. Get some rest. We start before first light.' Red Shirt melted away into the darkness.

Griffin overheard the report. 'Thirteen people, almost three-to-one odds, and we've the surprise advantage.' Waco smiled without pleasure. Griffin could just make out his features. 'You mean to have your revenge for the last time?'

Waco nodded. 'I do, I've told the men McGee's mine.'

'So long as he's dead, I don't care,' said Griffin.

They wrapped themselves into their blankets and tried to sleep. Hours later, Red Shirt woke Waco, and he roused the others. Without coffee or breakfast, tempers were short and arguments broke out. 'You men save it,' said Waco. 'There'll be plenty of fightin' soon enough. Now fork your horses.'

They crested the ridge to the south and east of the ranch house; it was still dark.

Even though Red Shirt scouted the valley, Waco did not intend to make the mistake he made the first time. He halted a quarter mile from the house and had the men dismount. 'OK, hobble your horses here. We go in on foot.'

Again, the men grumbled; one spoke out. 'Why can't we just ride down shootin'?'

Waco's temper had grown short. 'Cause the last time, they was waitin' for us. They killed ten of us afore we knew what was happenin'. We're goin' to ease down there quiet like, get into position, and them give 'em hell – got it? Remember what I said, the redhead is mind.'

They strung out, forming a semi-circle that enveloped the buildings: house, barn, and bunkhouse. The signal was the first shot from Waco's gun. He studied the house. As before, the house was dark and there was no movement. Something didn't feel right. Hell, it was too late now.

He aimed at the front door and fired.

Griffin watched from the ridge; the dawn was still grey, and he could make out the flashes of the gunshots; it was pure bedlam. The shots were three-to-one from Waco and his men, but the ranchers' rate of return fire didn't seem to diminish.

Were they somehow warned we were coming?

I bet it was Potts, no, Miller. It had to be him. I'll take care of that son-of-a-bitch when this is over. Potts too if he gives me any trouble.

The sun peeked above the trees and flooded across the valley. Puffs of grey smoke replaced muzzle flashes and began to collect into a low-hanging cloud, neither side gaining an advantage.

Movement across the vale caught Griffin's eye. Riders streamed over the ridge on the far side. As they rode down into the valley, they spread into a line, a line of death. A quick glance back to Waco confirmed his attention was on the battle, and the din concealed the noise of riders coming.

Spellbound, Griffin watched as, one-by-one, the men sensed the coming of the riders. He imagined he could see the fear in their wild-eyed stares as they sprang to their feet. They threw lead at the riders, but none hit a mark. They fell where they stood, each shot by either the approaching riders, or the shooters firing from the ranch.

Soon the shooting stopped; he wondered if any of them lived.

Devastated, he pulled back from his vantage place on the ridge, mounted his horse, and rode away.

CHAPTER 16

Six men survived the onslaught of the ranchers' charge from the west. Since there was no law in Charlo to deal with them, they were patched up and sent on their way to live or die on the trail.

Roberts and the others came to the house. 'Are you folks all right?'

Helen came out on to the porch. 'Yes, very well, thanks to you gentlemen. I'll never be able to repay you, you've saved our lives.'

Updike stepped to the edge of the porch. 'Mrs Baxter, it's we who owe you. Had we banded together when Griffin began his shenanigans your husband and son might still be alive.'

Her smile was tightlipped, but genuine. 'Let's hear no more about the subject, Mr Updike. It's in the past. Now we've the chance to start over.'

'I would take it as a sign of a beginning friendship if you'd call me Jeremy.'

'If you'll address me as Helen,' she said.

He smiled warmly. 'I shall, Helen, thank you.'

Warren said his goodbyes and headed home with his men. 'I got cattle needs tendin' and the missus worries,' he said with his departure.

Spooner was next, and then Roberts left; Updike lingered. 'I would be happy to stay here until your Mr McGee returns. Besides, after all that Roberts told me, I would very much like to meet him.'

Flustered, her face blushed, and she said, 'I'm afraid that I – we – don't have the accommodation to house you and your men.'

'Think nothing of it, Helen,' said Updike. 'I've my tent, and the men are used to sleeping rough as it were.'

Helen and Sarah entertained Mr Updike for two evenings. On the morning of the third day after the gun battle, Sarah saw cattle slowly crest the west side of the valley. Soon a lone figure galloped toward the house and her.

She was off the porch running across the yard to meet him. Toots jumped from the saddle as Knothead slid to a halt. They embraced tightly, and then he held her at arm's length. 'Are you all right, Sarah? We run into Mr Roberts and his men, and he told me what happened.'

She beamed at him. 'Now that you're home, I couldn't be better.' She looked past him at the cattle. 'They look in pretty bad shape. How many did you find?'

'Close to a hundred. They was hid in a small grassy canyon. They had plenty of water, but the grass was gone when we got there. Whoever was tendin' 'em lit out when we showed up, so there weren't no gunplay. They're weak, so we drove 'em home slow, lettin' 'em graze on whatever they could find along the way. Once they fatten up we'll have the beginnin's of a herd.'

Sarah's brow pinched as she looked away. 'You know, William, when Pap was still alive we had better 'an 4,000 head. I wonder what Griffin done with 'em?'

Toots did the math. 'Hell's bells, Sarah, that's near one hundred sixty thousand dollars on the hoof.' Then as if it had just appeared, Toots saw Updike's campsite. 'What's all that?' He pointed.

'Oh,' said Sarah. 'That's Mr Jeremy Updike. He's one of the ranchers who came to help us. I think he's sweet on Mama.'

Toots grinned. 'How's Gus taken it?'

Sarah giggled as she took one of Toots's hands into hers. 'He's grumpy now that you mention it. I know he's sweet on Mama too.'

'I don't expect he figures anything to come of it, but he is particular about your mother, and I think she knows it too.'

Sarah's expression hardened and she stood very erect. 'Mother has done nothing inappropriate.'

Toots laughed. 'I know that, no need to take offense.'

She relaxed and tucked herself under his arm and they started toward the house. Helen and Mr Updike walked out to meet them.

Updike stepped forward with his hand extended. 'I am so very pleased to meet you, Mr McGee.'

Toots accepted his hand and held on as Updike pumped it with great enthusiasm. At length, Toots said, 'The pleasure is mind, sir. Accordin' to Mr Roberts, it was you who led the charge down on the gunmen.'

Helen stared up at him. 'Is that true, Jeremy?'

Updike looked cornered. 'Don't make too much of that, Helen. It was rather cowardly on my part. Those poor men didn't have a chance really.'

Toots said, 'Oh, I forgot they was unarmed and couldn't shoot at you.'

'Well, I. . . .'

Helen took his arm. 'Thank you, Jeremy.'

Updike stared at Toots, admiration in his eyes. 'Mr Roberts says many good things about you, sir, and I wanted to make your acquaintance. You must tell me all about yourself and how you found yourself here embroiled in a range war.'

Sarah turned to Toots. 'Yes I'd like to know all too.'

Supper was a hearty affair; the best that Chen knew how to prepare. The group talked until late into the night. The evening ended with a toast to their collective futures.

At first light, Toots was alone on the road to Charlo. He had business with Griffin. His hold on the Box-B ended today.

When Toots arrived, the townsfolk were busy with their morning routines. Murphy swept the entrance to his store, Page walked across the street to the café; it was too early for the saloon to be open. Various shop owners milled about their shops getting ready for the days hoped-for business.

He reined in at the livery. Jenkins, the owner sat on a stump near the entrance puffing on his clay pipe drinking coffee. His eyes twinkled and he smiled at Toots as he knocked out the hot coal. 'Been expectin' ya. It's still early. Want some Arbuckle?'

Toots stepped down and draped the reins over the fence rail. He felt old, or at least how he thought old would feel. He was tired of the fighting, the strain of worry, and being on constant guard. 'Thank you, Mr Jenkins, I believe I will.'

Unsolicited, Jenkins said, 'Griffins is expectin' ya too. He's been holed up in his office since the shootin' out at your place.'

'Anybody with 'im?'

'Not that I saw, but he's a sneaky bastard. Better watch your back.'

Toots nodded. 'Sort of figured—'

'You want some company? I'd be proud to help.'

A warm, gentle smile crossed Toots's face. 'I appreciate the offer, old-timer, but I figured I'd handle him alone.'

Jenkins nodded and set to repacking his pipe. 'Leave your horse here. I'll take care of 'im till you're ready to go.'

'Thanks,' said Toots as he handed back the empty tin cup. 'I guess it's time.' He loosened his Colt, pulled down his hat, and started off toward Griffin's office.

People paused to stare as he walked past. Many ducked back into their businesses. Others, like Murphy, stopped what they were doing to watch.

At Griffin's office, Toots halted at the storefront window and gazed inside. The room was dim, and his clerk was absent; Griffin had the door to his office closed. He continued across the building to the alleyway that ran alongside. Toots peeked through the partially opened curtains on the office's rear entrance.

He saw Griffin at his desk staring at the interconnecting office door with a revolver in his hand. Griffin looked haggard; he was unkempt, and shabby.

Pulling his Colt with his right hand, Toots tried the doorknob with his left; it turned. In one smooth motion, Toots pushed open the door, stepped into the office, and cocked his revolver. The double clicks spoke its own command; Griffin froze.

'Empty your hand, Griffin. You're goin' to hang for the murder of Luke Baxter and his son. There are others, but we'll start with 'em.'

The gun clattered on the desktop. Griffin's shoulder dropped and he leaned back in his chair and hooked his thumbs into the vest pockets. 'You think you can prove that?'

'I do. Now, real slow, on your feet. You're goin' to jail.'

158

Griffin leered; his smile resembled a snake. 'We'll see, boy.'

As he stood, he straightened his clothes and smoothed his jacket. He paused at the door to finger-comb his hair before putting on his hat. In the dimmed light of the outer office, he palmed his Derringer from his vest.

He stopped abruptly before reaching the door, causing Toots to run into him. Toots's Colt poked into his back. 'Move, Griffin.'

Griffin whirled to his left knocking Toots's arm away. His right hand came forward as he cocked the Derringer. Toots saw a glint of light flash off the gun's barrel, and looped a haymaker with his left hand. The gun exploded into the air as Griffin staggered backwards.

Regaining his feet, Griffin readied for his second shot. Toots also recovered, and seeing the Derringer brought up his Colt with a yell. 'Don't do it!'

Griffin thrust his Derringer forward and fired. At the same instant, Toots pulled the Colt's trigger. In the small room, the boom of both guns discharging together was deafening.

With his arm extended, the recoil from the short-barreled gun kicked his arm upward and the slug slammed into the ceiling, causing plaster to fall like snow.

Toots's lead flew true and struck Griffin in the center of his chest. He sat down hard and glanced up at Toots, and then his Derringer. 'Guess Malone was right. . . .' He slumped forward, dead.

Murphy was the first to the office; he peered through the window, making eye contact with Toots before entering. 'You all right, McGee?' asked Murphy.

Page came next and then Judge Miller. He saw Griffin on the floor and the gun in Toots's hand. 'You're under arrest.'

Toots leveled the Colt and pulled back the hammer. 'What for, he fired twice. I had no choice.'

Murphy bent down and searched Griffin's body; the Derringer remained in his hand. He stood, broke the chamber, ejected the spent cartridges, and held them out for the judge. 'It appears to me that it was self-defense, Judge. Besides, you was goin' to arrest Griffin anyway for leading an ambush raid on the Box-B.'

'I haven't any proof,' said the judge. He gave Murphy a stern look as he straightened the lapels of his jacket.

Toots kept his Colt pointed at the judge. 'There's more 'an thirty graves at the ranch, countin' both raids. The survivors of the raid identified Griffin and Waco Turner as the leaders.'

Doc Benson pushed through the crowd to see if medical services were required. Overhearing Toots comment, he said, 'I got two of 'em over to my office right now. The young man is telling the truth, Judge.'

'Well, there still needs to be a formal coroner's inquest.'

Murphy stepped between Toots and the judge. 'Well, the whole town's here including the doc, so let's do it now, be done with this business, and get on with our lives.'

The crowd looked on expectantly; Miller shrugged. Twenty minutes later the judge said, 'I hereby declare this shooting justifiable homicide. Court adjourned.'

Toots paused at the door and looked back. 'Judge, Griffin stole near $160,000 worth of cattle from the Box-B. Who do I see about the money?' He lowered his hand to the butt of his Colt. 'I aim to get it back.'

160